To Fred;

From a slacker to an expert.

Marty Schabloff

Murder On The Dunes

Library of Congress Control Number: 2004110273

To order additional copies, please contact us.
BookSurge, LLC
www.booksurge.com
1-866-308-6235
orders@booksurge.com

MARTIN SOKOLOFF

MURDER ON THE DUNES

A NOVEL

2004

Murder On The Dunes

ACKNOWLEDGEMENTS

This book has essentially two histories. It was conceived in a class, The Mystery Novel, at the Academy for Lifelong Learning of Cape Cod Community College. In that class taught by Professor Virginia Harvey, we were divided into groups and assigned the task of developing the outlines of a murder mystery, one mystery per group. My group came up with an outline of the story; the clues found during the investigation; names of the characters; the locale; and a few assorted facts to provide "corroborative detail intended to lend artistic verisimilitude to an otherwise bald and unconvincing narrative," to quote William S. Gilbert.

The class ended, the materials we developed remained in my file, untouched, untended, and ignored, for about ten years. I am grateful to Professor Harvey for inspiring my group and myself to work to produce the basic structure of a book and for helping me to understand how a mystery story is developed.

The book was born in a subsequent course, Writers Group, led by David Acker, in the same Academy for Lifelong Learning, about two years ago. Up until that time in that class, I had been involved in writing my memoirs, and after being satisfied that I need no longer devote most of my attention to them, I looked around for a new project, and found my old notes on the mystery. Wow, I thought, here's a challenge! I decided to include all the details and bits of odds and ends from the original group, into a novel and try to make it hang together.

Because of the supportive environment that David Acker provided in class, as well as the inspiration of listening to his rendition of his poetry, both serious and humorous, each week, I came to the group prepared to present something I had written, until the book was complete.

Since that time, quite a few people have been of considerable help in moving the book from a raw manuscript to its final form, and I would like to express my gratitude to them.

To my daughter, Beth Sokoloff, who kept my computer under control when I couldn't, and for her encouraging feedback; to my daughter, Marjorie Allen, for digging through early versions of the manuscript, for questioning some of my workings of description and dialogue, for offering lots of encouragement; to my son, Stephen Sokoloff, for his feedback, and for legal advice when necessary. My daughter-in-law, Freddi Sokoloff gave me a push sometimes when it was necessary to keep me at it. Thanks also to Bill Wibel, for his behind-the-scenes activities, taking care of many details when they needed taking care of. Also thanks to Mark Allen for supplying me with many mystery story models as inspiration.

I am grateful to two fine police officers who were extremely patient with me and helped to dispel some of my ignorance about police procedures. They are Sergeant James Plath, of the Massachusetts State Police, Homicide Squad, and Sergeant Claire Benjamin of the Provincetown, Massachusetts Police Department. Both of them provided me with a great deal of background information about how the police operate in murder cases. If there are glaring errors in this story, they are exclusively mine.

When I was searching about for a cover picture for this book, Ann Corbett was kind enough to offer me the use of her beautiful watercolor painting, *Pamet Harbor,* which now graces the cover of this book. I am deeply grateful to her.

The staff of Book Surge was very helpful in supporting me throughout the publishing process, of which I was a naive novice. I thank Roy Francia, Sharon Crocker and Lyndsay Speirs for all their help.

Extra thanks go to Myka-Lynne Sokoloff who graciously undertook the final editing of this book, between periods of her own editing work. The text reads immeasurably better for her comments and suggestions. Testimonial to her tact and diplomacy lies in the fact that we are still friends.

And, finally, to my wife, Vivienne, for standing behind me as I frantically typed, reading the output, offering suggestions, telling me how great the story was, and providing the enthusiasm that kept me at the work until it was done.

BROOKLINE UNIVERSITY
Memorandum

Date: May 1, 2005
To: All Academic Deans
From: William Lodge, President
Re: New Promotion and Tenure Policy

The Board of Trustees of Brookline University, in order to attain the highest possible quality of faculty and courses of instruction, has adopted a policy that now will require all faculty who are not tenured or on a tenure track to make application to the University Committee on Tenure and Promotion.

Those non-tenured faculty who have served three or more years on the faculty either will be granted tenure according to the procedures of the Committee or their faculty appointments will be terminated at the end of next school year. I expect that you will carry out the appropriate actions necessary to ensure the success of this policy.

I recognize this action may create some hardship for a small number of faculty members, but I hope that the pride of contributing toward upgrading of this fine university will offer some compensation.

I wish you all a pleasant summer.

This Book Is Dedicated To All The "Teachers" Who Taught Me Most Of What I Know.

CHAPTER I

Hello, this is Professor Toro. Can I help you?"

"Good morning, Charles, this is Dean Rogers. I wonder whether you have a few minutes to meet with me over coffee in the Faculty Dining Room."

""What's it about, Fred? I can be there in about five minutes."

"Thanks, Charles. I'll tell you all about it when I see you. Five minutes, okay?"

"I'll be there."

Wonder what bee the old goat has in his proverbial this morning, thought Charles as he dropped the term paper he was reading on his desk and rose to leave his office.

Once in the dining room, Charles looked around. The room was reminiscent of many other academic environments, with wainscoted walls, tables covered with white cloths and deep carpeting on the floors. Charles found it easy to locate the dean, who was sitting at a table surrounded by a group of about ten faculty members, mostly young, all of them hanging on the dean's every word, laughing at some story he was recounting in an Irish dialect.

As soon as he saw Charles, Dean Rogers cut his story short and suggested to Charles that they move to a secluded, unoccupied table nearby. They filled their cups from the large urn at the end of the dining room and moved to the table the dean had indicated.

"What's on your mind, Fred?" asked Toro.

The dean watched as Toro emptied precisely three packages of sugar into his coffee cup. Finally, as Charles tasted his coffee and seemed satisfied, the dean cleared his throat and began, somewhat hesitantly. "You know, our new president is out to make Brookline University a high prestige school and is on the asses of all the deans and department heads to upgrade the qualifications of their respective faculties."

"Well, my feeling is that this school is a sow's ear, and nothing President Lodge can do will make a 'high prestige' silk purse out of it," said Charles testily.

"Your opinion isn't relevant," said Rogers. " You probably know that the president has set up a committee on promotions and tenure to review all faculty upgrades."

"What has that to do with me?"

"Well, the president specifically told me that he wants your name submitted to the committee for consideration for promotion from assistant professor to associate. He also said that since you're not on a tenure track, if the committee turns you down, you'll be terminated at the end of next year."

"So, what am I supposed to do about it?" Charles demanded.

"The committee will be looking primarily at three criteria: the quality of your graduate training, evaluations from your chairman and students, and your recent record of publications. I would doubt whether any scholar east of the Mississippi would ever have heard of your graduate school, and your list of publications is so short as to be nonexistent. As for "good" or "excellent" evaluations, I'd have to look long and hard to find any. So the pressure will be on you to get yourself published before the committee meets next February. I'd suggest you don't teach any summer courses; just spend the summer working on your research."

"You know there isn't the chance of a snowball in hell of my getting something published by February!"

"Well, you'll either have something accepted for publication by then, or start looking around for another job," said Rogers. "By the way, weren't you talking last year about possibly researching that twelve thousand-year-old settlement they uncovered on Coast Guard Beach on the Cape?"

"Yes, I thought about it, but decided not to, and then I turned the idea over to one of my graduate students as a subject for his master's thesis. I guess I'll have to think of something else."

As he returned to his office, Toro's mind was occupied by a single thought: *How can I get my name on that master's study that young man —Robert Benton —is writing?*

Two weeks later, Professor Toro was sitting in his office, engaged in conversation with two of his advisees, Diana Wellman and Robert Benton. Of the two, Diana was the prettier: blonde, curly hair, azure blue eyes, and a splendid figure, top to bottom. By contrast Bobby was dark: dark hair, dark eyes, and a dark complexion, but women found him handsome.

Diana was dressed in a fairly form-fitting blue sweater, a plaid skirt that effected a compromise between too short and barely sufficient, and penny loafers. Bobby was, in his own estimation, overdressed in an oxford, button-down shirt, somewhat rumpled jeans, and sandals.

"Mr. Benton," said Toro, "I've given your report a thorough going over, and, while your basic idea is good, the whole project needs to be fleshed out a great deal."

"I'm not sure I understand what you mean, Professor Toro. Last month you said the paper was almost ready to go to the rest of my committee."

"What I mean, Robert, is that there are some sections in the paper that are only backed up by a scanty amount of on-the-ground research and that it needs more work at the site."

"But," said Bobby, "they told me that I couldn't spend any more time at the site; there are other students who need access to it. How am I supposed to get more work done there?"

"I think I can help you to answer that question. I've been in contact with the people at the site and they're willing to have you back there as long as we're working together. What we can do is to share authorship of the project, and, with me as the senior author, you'll have the full authority of the university behind you in getting whatever access you'll still need at the site."

"Are you saying what I'm thinking you're saying, that you want to take credit for my work? And pass it off as yours?"

"That's not at all what I'm saying, Bobby. What I'm suggesting is that we form a partnership, with you doing the site work and writing up your results in rough form, and then I'll polish up and clean up what you've done. Put it in final form, as you might say. And then it'll stand a good chance of getting published if it has my name at the top. With yours right underneath, of course."

"I never heard of anything so ridiculous!" shouted Bobby.

At this moment neither Robert nor Toro paid any heed to Diana, who was showing signs of acute anxiety. Her face turned red, her breaths became shallow and more rapid, tears welled up in her eyes, and she slid down in her chair, as though by doing that, she would become invisible.

"I'm sure you'll think better of my offer after you've had a chance to cool down and consider your alternatives. I carry weight with your committee and you can be sure they will give your thesis very favorable consideration if we've worked together," Toro added.

"Tell me, Professor, do things like this go on at all universities, or only here at Brookline?"

"Well, Robert, part of our mission is to train students to survive in the real world. You might consider this an important part of your reality training."

"C'mon, Diana, let's get out of here before I say or do something I'll regret later."

"Bobby, I'll meet you later," Diana responded with hesitation. "Professor Toro has offered me some work helping him with the manuscript he'll be writing in Provincetown this summer."

"What do you mean, you'll be working for him? Does that include staying with him?" Bobby turned to Toro, "What kinds of plans do you have for Diana at your little 'love nest'?"

With this, Diana yanked the engagement ring off her finger, threw it at Bobby and shouted, "If that's all the trust you have in me, forget our engagement!"

Bobby picked up the ring, stuffed it in his pants pocket, and stormed out of the room.

CHAPTER II

Police Chief Dennis Dawes was sitting in his office in Provincetown Police Headquarters in a former funeral home, wondering what in hell he was doing there. *Of all the jobs I could have taken, this is probably one of the worst. The Town Council is always complaining about the crime rate. The tourists —maybe half of them —come here to raise one kind of hell or another. My officers are all unhappy about no new contract or pay raises. Every once in a while I get to hating this town, and today is one of those days. Even this damn bubble gum tastes awful.*

Nothing seems to be going right, he mused. *This weekend we're having the Blessing of the Fleet. The town, if everybody isn't already going crazy counting out all the money they're gonna make, will be on my tail to make sure my officers keep their shops and galleries and restaurants well patrolled and safe. If that isn't enough, we've got those visitors loving coming here and trying to find a parking place. If, and when, they get back to their cars and find their tires slashed, I'm the one who gets blamed.*

Having somewhat vented his spleen, Dennis leaned back in his swivel chair and contemplated another reality of his existence. *P'town* he thought, *is really a great place. Where else can you find a place that is as free and open and accepting as here? Walk down Commercial Street and in less than two minutes you can see a greater variety of people than you could imagine: gay and lesbian couples walking hand in hand; street people; wildly dressed visitors from all over; yuppie families, dressed in the latest from Abercrombie and Banana Republic, their kids licking ice cream cones and cotton candy; fishermen in jeans, boots and sweat shirts; young people walking bicycles; cars and trucks creeping along the main streets looking, hopelessly, for a parking space. And almost everybody getting along on the crowded streets and sidewalks with little or no friction.*

Dennis looked down at as much of himself as he could see without a full-length mirror. Unpressed khaki shirt and pants did not seem too impressive by way of a uniform. A wide brown leather belt with a large buckle depicting several sailboats under full sail added whatever distinction his outfit afforded. It surely was not his ratty, old, but comfortable work boots, or the equally ratty, old Greek fisherman's hat, which reposed on his desk. The only indication of his occupation or rank was his police chief's badge, which he wore pinned to his left breast pocket. A large, rather scraggly moustache covered his upper lip, while heavy brows shaded his eyes, which were medium brown. Topping all this was a head of dark brown hair, increasingly mixed with gray, which did not seem overly combed. Altogether, Dennis Dawes presented the image of a refugee from a Goodwill thrift shop.

At this moment his intercom buzzed. It took a moment for Dennis to bring himself back into the present. Finally he growled into the intercom, "Yeah?"

"There's a Mrs. Benton here who wants to see you, desperately, it seems."

"Give me a minute, Dot, and then show her in, please"

After making an abortive attempt to neaten the top of his desk, the chief got to his feet, moved out from behind his desk and greeted his visitor, a very attractive woman who looked to be in her middle forties, or, perhaps, her early fifties. (Dennis was not the best judge of a woman's age.)

In contrast to most women in Provincetown at that time of year, she was immaculately dressed in a freshly ironed faded denim shirt with flowers embroidered down the front closure, a dark blue denim mid-calf length skirt, and what looked like expensive sandals on her feet. Her dark brown eyes seemed to have been designed to match her dark brown hair, which came down slightly below her shoulders. With a small mouth, slightly upturned at the corners and a small nose, also upturned, she was, at least to Dennis, a very attractive woman.

Without knowing why, Dennis got the perception that Mrs.

Benton was used to getting things done, and getting them done her way. The chief's secretary, Dot, followed her into the office, and Dennis asked Dot to bring in some coffee.

"How do you take it, Mrs. Benton?" asked Dot.

"Just black, please."

As they both sat down, Dennis asked Mrs. Benton what he could do to help her. "I'm not sure what you can do to help, but let me tell you why I'm here."

At that moment Dot came in balancing two mugs of coffee. She handed one to Mrs. Benton, the other to the chief, and stood there waiting for the conversation to continue, looking first at Mrs. Benton, then at Dennis.

"Thank you, Dot, that will be all." Reluctantly, Dot turned and slowly walked out the door.

"The reason I'm here," began Mrs. Benton, "is that my son has disappeared, and I have reason to believe that he is here, somewhere in Provincetown. He was terribly upset the last time I saw him, and I'm afraid he might be in some kind of danger."

Then, tears appeared in her eyes, and she looked around for something to use to wipe them. Dennis reached across his desk and handed her a box of tissues. She pulled one loose, daintily wiped her nose and looked up at Dennis.

"Tell me, Mrs. Benton, why do you think he might be in danger?"

"Please call me Betty, and thank you for the tissue. I hope I won't need any more." She broke off and remained silent for a moment before beginning again, obviously struggling to regain her composure. "My son Bobby had a terrible fight with his advisor at his graduate school and with his fiancée, Diana. She broke off their engagement and told Bobby she was going to come here with the professor to help him work on his book. I guess that's why they had the fight. I'm sure Bobby came here looking for her. He has a terrible temper sometimes, and I'm concerned for him."

"What was Bobby's fight with his professor about, uh, Betty? Was it about Diana?"

"No, and yes. Mostly it was about the master's thesis Bobby is working on. He was studying an archeological site here on the Cape. Apparently a storm on Coast Guard Beach uncovered remains of an ancient culture there; they think it was from about twelve thousand years ago."

"But what was the fight about?"

"Bobby thought he was almost finished with his work. Then the professor told him that it needed more work and that the professor was going to help him finish it and wanted to share authorship with Bobby. He was going to take most of the credit for the paper and give Bobby very little."

"From what you're saying, Betty, it looks like we need to worry about the professor, not Bobby so much."

"Why, what do you mean?"

"Well, if someone was trying to steal my research, *and* my girl friend, I don't think I'd be terribly concerned with *his* welfare. I might even consider taking some action against him."

"Oh, I don't think Bobby is capable of violence. I just don't know why, but I have this feeling that he's in some kind of danger, and I can't feel comfortable until I know he's okay. What can you do to help me?"

"If you can give my secretary a thorough description of your son, we can have all our police officers on the lookout for him. Also give her the professor's address here on the Cape. By the way, what's *his* name?"

"Professor Charles Toro. From the Archaeology department at Brookline University. He must be a terrible man."

"Well, I'm sure that Bobby is all right. I'll have my officers looking for him within a few minutes. Why don't you check back with me later this afternoon? And, by the way, this is the weekend of the Blessing of the Fleet here in town and the town's hoping for lots of tourists, even though only the locals usually turn out in any numbers. So be careful. Where are you staying?"

"No place yet, I thought I'd just find Bobby and have him come back to Boston with me. Now it doesn't all seem that simple."

"Dot can help you find a place. She'll help you get in touch with the Chamber of Commerce, if you'd like."

"Oh, thank you. You've been very helpful, and I really appreciate it."

"No problem, Betty, it's part of my job. Happy if I can be of some help. Don't forget to check back with me later. Please leave Bobby's picture with Dot on your way out, and give her a description of him that's as specific as you can."

Dennis waited a minute after Betty left, and then broke out in a series of expletives that might have disturbed the equanimity of an eighteenth-century buccaneer. "Another missing kid case! That only makes about twelve this week! I've got to quit this job!" Then, to himself he added, *That Betty Benton is a pretty nice woman. I wonder if she is connected with anyone. I can always ask her to have dinner with me tonight when she checks back about her son. Okay, why not?*

Out came the pack of bubble gum. The chief slipped out a stick and tossed it into his mouth. "God, that tastes awful!"

CHAPTER III

The harbor was full of boats on moorings, lazily bobbing up and down with the gentle wavelets which rippled in from the bay. The sky was an azure blue, occasionally dotted with a small, fair weather cloud of a puffy white consistency, which looked somewhat like a ball of absorbent cotton.

This is really a picturesque place to visit, Betty was thinking as she walked along, right near the water, looking for Brewer's Dune Taxi. She'd been told that he generally parked in a space just opposite the Macmillan Wharf parking lot.

If not for Bobby's disappearing, I could really enjoy being here. As soon as I get some time, I want to walk out on Macmillan's Wharf and look at the fishing boats. Those men on the boats are really brave to go out in those rough seas and handle those big nets. And some of them are pretty sexy looking, with their strong arms and bare bronzed chests! Just then Betty noticed a beat-up old, green suburban parked along the curb, with *Brewer's Dune Taxi* painted on the sides. The seats were dirty and worn; the dash was buried in used cardboard cups and cigarette butts.

"Are you Mr. Brewer?" Betty asked the somewhat scruffy-looking man who was lounging against the taxi.

"Nope, but he's having coffee at John's Cafe, over on Commercial Street. You can find him there, if you don't take too long."

A few minutes later, Betty walked into John's so-called Cafe, looked around, and decided she really didn't want to be there; still, she realized she'd have to bear the flies, the smell of stale beer, the dirty dishes and crumbs on the tables, if she wished to talk to Brewer. Only one table was occupied, and Betty walked over to it somewhat hesitatingly, addressing the man sitting there. "I beg your pardon, are you Mr. Brewer?"

He slowly looked up at her, giving her a view of unshaven cheeks, a mouth from which several teeth were missing, and a pair of eyes that could be tritely described as bloodshot. Betty noticed that in spite of the warm weather, he was wearing a plaid flannel button-down shirt from which the buttons were largely absent, rumpled jeans, and ratty sneakers. "Yeah, I'm Jack Brewer. What can I do for you? This ain't my office hours, you know? This here's my coffee break."

"I'm very sorry to disturb your break, Mr. Brewer, but I need to talk to you. I need to rent your taxi for a while to go out on the dunes."

"Oh, that's what you want. I thought you might be looking for something else. Right now I'm all out of that. Tell me what you want, specifically."

"Well, I'm not sure. I think my son may be at one of the dune shacks that his professor is renting for the summer, and I need to see him desperately. I've been told that you know all about the dunes, and the shacks, and you could help me find him."

"Probably I can, but what did they tell you about how much it will cost? My taxi rents out for twenty-five bucks an hour, and for special work like you want, my services run another twenty-five."

"I don't care how much, I just want to find Bobby!" After a deep breath, she said more calmly, "Okay, tell me what we have to do."

"Okay, sit down and let's talk. Tell me everything about this."

Betty sat down and started to tell Brewer all about Bobby and Diana and the professor, leaning close so that the bartender couldn't overhear.

Just then Dennis Dawes walked in. Seeing the two of them with their heads close together in what looked like some sort of intimacy, Dennis turned red, muttered something about looking for tire slashers, spun around and stomped out onto the street. Betty jumped up from the table, told Brewer she'd catch up with him later, and ran out. She looked up and down Commercial Street and finally caught sight of Dennis about two blocks away, walking toward the Town Hall building. Half running and half walking rapidly, she caught up with him, and took hold of his arm.

"Dennis, please, listen to me."

"I guess you don't want to have dinner with me tonight."

"Dinner? Were we supposed to have dinner? Did you ask me to have dinner with you tonight?"

"Oh, damn, I was meaning to ask you when you checked back with me later this afternoon. Looks like you won't be needing *my* help any longer."

"That's not true. Please, I was just talking to Jack about renting his taxi to take me out to the dunes to look for Bobby. I think Bobby must be out there looking for Diana. Did you really intend to ask me to dinner?"

"Well."

"Because, if you did, I'd love to have dinner with you."

"Oh, I'll be there. See you at five. Meet me at my office." Dennis turned again toward the town hall, while Betty returned to John's Cafe.

As he turned to enter Town Hall, the chief noticed two men hastily move around the corner about half a block away. He immediately began to walk rapidly in their direction, breathing very hard after walking only a few steps. He was thinking, irreverently, *Now would be a good time to make some 'heavy breathing' phone calls.* After a few minutes, Dennis caught up with the pair, and hailed them.

"Hold it, guys. I want a few words with you."

The pair consisted of Joe Stabile and Frank Barnes, a couple of locals frequently found on the fringes of the Provincetown populace known more for their slightly criminal activities than their good works. They began to shift slightly in their stances, and avoided any semblance of eye contact with the police chief. Joe seemed to have been elected head spokesman for the pair, who almost never were seen separately and who most people thought were joined at the hip.

"Chief, we ain't done nothin'."

"Who said you did?"

"Aw, c'mon, Chief, anytime something bad happens around town, you're always blamin' us."

"And I can't think of a more likely couple of guys. And, while we're just talking, I've had a number of complaints from visitors that their car tires have been slashed. You two know anything about that?"

"Why, Chief, you know we'd never do nothin' like that!"

"Oh, sure. But let me tell you, we have a big weekend coming up. Lots of visitors in town, and I don't want to hear a word about a single tire being slashed, or any other malicious mischief being pulled, or I'll have your butts decorating my office wall!"

"Hey, Chief, our hands are as clean as the driven snow. You won't have any trouble from us. Scout's honor."

God! Thought Dennis, *what have the scouts come to now!*

CHAPTER IV

Diana, dear, you shouldn't be so worried. You were absolutely right to break off your engagement to that hotheaded young man. Come on, relax and we'll have a glass of wine before dinner."

As he spoke, Charles Toro was opening a jug of California Cabernet and having difficulty unscrewing the metal cap. The two of them were in Charles' rental shack out on the Province Lands dunes, ostensibly working on his manuscript.

Hoping to distract the professor and reacting to her feeling that she'd made a mistake in coming to this place, Diana asked, "These dune shacks are very special, aren't they, although to me it seems just like a shack?"

"Yes, Diana, this is one of the cottages that were privately owned before the National Seashore Park was established. Then the government took them over by eminent domain when the park was formed. Now the government rents them out. I sublet this one from a friend of a friend who has the contract for this one. We're very lucky to have one of them. The rumor is that the National Park may take them over and rent them out to new people. The present occupants are up in arms. But we won't worry our little heads about them, will we? Now, here is your wine, drink up."

"But, Professor, don't we have to do some work on your book?"

"Oh, come on, Diana, it's time to unwind and have a little fun for a while before we start working. Here, this wine will get you in the right spirit." He handed Diana the glass and rested his hand on her shoulder.

"Oh, Professor, I'm not sure we should be doing this. I'm

beginning to wonder if I did the right thing by coming here. And, since there's no telephone I don't know how I'll get a taxi to get back to my motel."

"Don't worry, baby, I have an extra cot, and, if worst comes to worst, you can always sleep there tonight." As he said this, Charles slid his hand down onto Diana's breast. At that instant, the front door opened with a crash, and in rushed Bobby.

"What's going on here? ... I guess I don't really have to ask. I'm sorry to interrupt your proceedings, but I need to talk to the professor, here."

"Robert Benton, there were no proceedings, and you'd do better cleaning your dirty mind. And, besides, I'm glad you're here. You can take me back to my motel."

"Not before I've had a chance to get this off my chest. *Mister* Toro, I've decided to go ahead on my thesis on my own. I've sent the dean a letter asking for a change in my advisor, and I won't be needing you to be involved any more. Diana, are you ready to leave now, or do you want to stay here and continue what you were doing before I walked in?"

"Please, Bobby, I want to go with you." They walked out together.

When they were in Bobby's rental SUV driving along a winding, sand-covered trail between the dunes, Diana snuggled closer to Bobby, who deliberately moved as far away as he could, a matter of about two inches. They were both silent for a long time.

Then Diana began. "Bobby, I'm so sorry that I behaved so badly. I never should have taken Professor Toro's offer of a job, especially when I heard that it involved working with him out here, alone on the dunes. I must have been crazy to agree."

"I'm sorry, Diana, but that's not good enough. The two of you looked pretty cozy there together when I walked in on you. I don't think I'm ready to forgive you. In fact, I'm not ready at all."

"Bobby, please! I didn't give him any encouragement. You're completely mistaken about what you think you saw when you burst in."

"I'm not sure about that. Just your being there was some amount of encouragement. Anyway, here we are at your motel. Good night!"

"Please come in for a while. We need to talk. I love you, Bobby, and I don't want us to end like this!"

"Well, I'll probably call you in the morning. Should I call you here, or at Professor Toro's?"

"That was a really low blow. Please call me here if you're interested. Good night." She jumped out of the car, and ran in the front door of the motel, tears streaming down her cheeks.

At the same time, seated in John's Cafe, Jack Brewer leaned over the table in almost whispered conversation with a young man about the same age as Bobby. In contrast to Brewer, the young man was gaudily dressed in a tan silk cowboy-style shirt. Under his collar was a bolo tie, with a large agate slide and the gold head of a steer embedded in the agate. He wore obviously brand new jeans with sharply pressed creases, a broad leather belt whose silver buckle repeated the steer's head on his tie. A brilliantly shining pair of alligator skin cowboy boots completed his outfit.

The young man had a thick head of black hair, neatly trimmed. His eyes were as black as his hair, his face somewhat a thin oval shape, with a pronounced nose and mouth. People who knew them both had difficulty distinguishing between Bill Phillips and his cousin Robert Benton. Women generally considered Bill handsome, but something about his manner made them cautious about getting involved with him in a romantic way.

"Bill," hissed Brewer, "When am I going to get that package? My customers are already after me."

"Don't worry, there's a shipment due outside of the harbor at ten tonight, and with all the fishing boat crews getting drunk tonight because of today's Blessing we don't have to worry too much about the Harbor Patrol. I hired those two jokers, Joe and Frank, to rent a boat and row out to meet the delivery boat at ten thirty, so I'll have the stuff probably by eleven at the latest. Meet me at Saylor's then and we can deal."

Raising himself from his chair, and looking around disdainfully, Bill Phillips strode out of the cafe and headed down toward the town hall. Passing the hall he continued another several blocks, turned right for half a block, and entered a house.

He climbed the stairs to the converted attic on the second floor, opened the door to his room and entered. He walked to a window at the front of the room and looked out over the waterfront. Bill could see the lights from several sailboats moored or anchored out in the harbor. Although not a sailor, or boater of any kind, he couldn't help admiring the graceful lines of some of the boats he could just about make out, out on the water.

Boy, wouldn't I love to be on one of those boats, sailing wherever I liked, instead of being cooped up in this lousy dump with no real past and no real future. I wouldn't have those hoods from Boston on my back to pay them for those last two shipments that ended up in the drink. Well, wishing isn't going to get me very far. We'd better do a better job on what's coming in tonight. Time to get ready to meet those two creeps.

He removed his cowboy outfit and donned a white tee shirt, a pair of well-bleached, worn jeans and a pair of Docksiders whose soles were worn down at the toes and heels. He stood thinking for a couple of minutes, then having obviously reached a decision, reached into a drawer, took out a black-handled knife in a sheath and strapped the sheath to his belt. He looked at himself in the mirror on the back of his door, sneered at his reflection, and walked out the door.

CHAPTER V

Some time later, in Saylor's Boat Yard, our two worthies Stabile and Barnes were discussing the rental of a dinghy with Al Saylor, the owner: "C'mon, Al, we just need it for a couple of hours to row out to one of the lobster boats out near Wood End. The most we can pay you is twenty-five bucks."

"You're asking me to let you two rent my best dinghy for God knows how long, for only twenty-five! I'll tell you what, there's that old beat-up wooden dory I can let you have for thirty. Take it or leave it!"

"Okay, we'll take it. Thanks for nothin'. We'll remember this when we get in the chips."

The three of them walked out of the office, down the yard to an ancient wooden dock, at the end of which the dory in question was tied. Al Saylor opened the top of a storage box lying on the dock. He took out a pair of oars and a pair of oarlocks and handed them to Joe Stabile.

"Here. Make sure you bring that dory back by seven tomorrow morning. Let's have the thirty dollars now."

Without a word, but accompanied by a villainous look, Stabile handed over a collection of crumpled, worn bills. Saylor silently counted them and turned and walked back to his office. Stabile climbed down into the dory, sat down on the center thwart, and fitted the oarlocks and oars in place. Frank Barnes then released the painter and climbed down into the dory, stepping past Joe and seating himself on the thwart at the aft end of the dory. Joe picked up the oars and began to row. Silently, except for the sound of the oars, the dory slipped past the end of the dock, and out toward the distant point.

CHAPTER VI

In the Chief's office, a resplendent Dennis was looking in a small mirror he usually kept in the back of his desk drawer. Having checked his slightly thinning hair, he moved down to his drooping, bushy moustache, and gave that a few downward swipes with the side of his index finger. His freshly shaved face was lightly scented by his bay rum after- shave lotion. Not having the benefit of a full-length mirror, he tried his best to get a view of the rest of his appearance: clean, open-collared button-down shirt of tan oxford; neatly pressed brown beltless slacks; light camel hair sport coat; brown tassel loafers; no socks.

Wonder if I should really wear a tie. No, she'll think I'm not up on what's the latest in casual.

Just then Dot buzzed and ushered Betty in without waiting for a response from Dennis. She gave Dennis a mock expression of shock at his appearance and carefully closed the door after flashing Dennis a wink. Betty was still wearing what she had worn in the afternoon, but she had added a handsome silk scarf, worn tied loosely over one shoulder.

"I'm sorry I couldn't dress appropriately for such an auspicious occasion," she said in a slightly flirtatious tone, "but I only have the clothes I left Boston in early this morning, although I did pick up a few 'necessaries'."

"You look great! I wouldn't worry, you'll have all the guys at the Red Inn popping their eyeballs out over you!" As he said this, Dennis thought to himself, "Hey, slow down, you've seen and dated pretty women before."

"Well, aren't you the gallant hero?" responded Betty.

Dennis coughed a couple of times, then said, "I think we'd

better get going. We have a reservation for six-thirty. That will just give us time for a couple of cocktails before dinner."

He took her arm and ushered her out of the office, ran back to his desk for just a second to deposit a wad of bubble gum from his mouth into the wastebasket next to his desk, then walked out and joined Betty.

"What would you like to drink?" asked Dennis. They were seated at a window table in the Red Inn, a restaurant overlooking Provincetown Harbor, each of them busy with her or his own thoughts. Betty was wondering how the evening would go, and how far. Dennis was hungrily looking out at the sailboats moored out in the harbor and wondering what it would be like to take this lady sailing on his own boat, which was one of those out in the harbor sailing gently back and forth on its mooring. The fantasy continued after the boat was anchored and the pair was below in the cabin, and then...then, Dennis decided he'd better come back to the present.

"I think I'll stick to white wine," Betty replied, "most alcohol makes me drowsy and relaxed to the point of wanting nothing more than going to bed."

"I wouldn't touch that statement with a pole of any length," said Dennis. He examined the wine list and turned to the waiter. "We'll have a bottle of the '89 Pouilly Fume, well chilled, please. And we'll order our food in a little while." To Betty he said "You never told me, were you able to get a room for tonight? Was Dot able to help you with some ideas?"

"She was a wonderful help! She helped me to get a beautiful room in a lovely B & B. I'd like to show it to you after we're through with dinner."

Thoughts, or rather fantasies—some visual, some auditory, some tactile—collided in Dennis's mind. He cleared his throat several times before continuing the conversation.

"Couple of my officers thought they had found your son. It seems there is a young fellow—his name is Bill Phillips—who resembles Bobby quite closely. As a matter of fact he claims to be related to you. Do you know him?"

"Yes, sure. He's from a branch of my *late* husband's family. He's been on the verge of trouble with the law on several occasions. Yes, he and Bobby do resemble each other physically, but that's as far as it goes."

"I don't think I follow you."

"The two of them never got along, and they don't really like each other. But, I don't want to talk about that. I want to know more about you. You don't impress me as being a policeman type."

"No? And what type do I impress you as being?"

"Well, you seem to be quite cultured and well educated, not at all like I would expect your average policeman to be. Oh, God, I must be sounding like the biggest snob!"

"No, you don't. I think I can guess what you're trying to say. Maybe some time I'll let my so-called hair down and tell all. But you're right; I wasn't always a cop. Enough about me. To get back to Bobby, I have a feeling he's probably okay. I sent a couple of my officers out to the professor's place to question him. It seems that Bobby *and* Diana had both been there earlier today and left together. It sounds to me like they're back together again."

"If that's true, maybe they've gone back to Boston. I guess I can start relaxing, and really enjoy the rest of the evening. I have something to tell you; I guess I should have told you earlier. This afternoon I rode out with Mr. Brewer to Professor Toro's house (rather a shack I would say) looking for Bobby and Diana. No one was there, but the door was open, so we went in. There, on the table was a draft copy of Bobby's thesis, with some notes scrawled on it. It looked as though the Professor had been doing some rewriting on it."

Just then their waiter appeared, carrying a bottle of wine. He ceremoniously exhibited the label to Dennis, who didn't bother to look at it, but just nodded, whereupon the waiter, again with pomp and ceremony, whipped out a corkscrew, pulled the cork out of the bottle and placed it on the table in front of Dennis. Dennis ignored it. The waiter splashed a bit of wine into Dennis' glass. Dennis took a sip, tasted it, and nodded again. The waiter filled both glasses and set the bottle into an ice-filled bucket. He gave Dennis a sneer and strutted, rather than walked, away from the table.

Dennis raised his glass. "Here's hoping we find Bobby very soon."

"I'll drink to that!"

"So tell me, what did you do after you found the thesis?"

Well, I hate to say this, but I grabbed the paper and ran out of there and we drove back to town."

"Do you still have the paper?"

"Yes, but I don't know what I should do with it."

"I'd hold on to it and give it to Bobby, when we find him. He may need it to prove to the school what Toro was doing."

Back came the waiter and they focused their attention on ordering dinner.

At the same time, Diana and Bobby were having dinner in a small cafe on Commercial Street, and an animated discussion was in progress. Both of them had calmed down considerably and had changed from their city attire to a white tee shirt for Bobby, a pink oxford shirt for Diana and jeans for both. Apparently, foot covering was necessary in restaurants, but both of them merely met the requirement.

"Bobby," Diana was saying, "I know I'm not as smart as you. In fact, you know, without your help I'd never have been able to get by in graduate school, and I'm very grateful to you. And I certainly would never do anything to hurt you, or destroy our relationship.

"What you saw when you walked in to Professor Toro's house was his doing, and I was about to fight him off when you walked in. If you hadn't interrupted, I think he would have ended with a black eye, and I would have ended up walking back to town."

"I guess," Bobby rejoined, "I'm partly responsible. My damned temper got the best of me when I saw his hand on your breast, and you looking like you were mad at me for walking in right then. I certainly didn't give you the benefit of the doubt."

"Are we back together and engaged again?"

"Yes, and, Diana, I really do love you."

"Then can I have my ring back?"

"Oh, boy! I gave it to my cousin, Bill Phillips, to sell for me. I hope he hasn't sold it yet! Damn!"

"Please get it back, Bobby! It means a lot to me."

"Bill better not have sold it! I don't trust him as far as I can throw him. Don't worry; I'll get it back. I have a date to meet him at Saylor's Boat Yard at eleven-thirty tonight."

CHAPTER VII

By the time Betty and Dennis reached her rooming house, and climbed up the stairs to her room, Betty was thinking, "I should never have had that glass of cognac after all that wine. I don't even remember whether I invited Dennis up to my room, or he just came as a matter of course."

"Betty, are you sure you're all right?"

"Yes, why do you ask?"

"Well, you invited me up here, but I'm not sure whether that was you or the alcohol talking."

"If you need convincing, I'll ask you again tomorrow morning." With that, Betty untied the scarf she was wearing, began fumbling with the buttons on her denim shirt, stopped and said, "If you think I'm so drunk and helpless, how about giving me a hand?"

"I think I can do better than that!" Dennis put his arms around her and kissed her, first on her mouth, then in her mouth, then down her neck and throat. His hands rapidly became busy, unbuttoning the rest of her shirt buttons and slipping the shirt off her shoulders, then unfastening the waist of her skirt, which slipped down to the floor.

Betty unhooked her bra and let it fall to the floor, and stepped out of her underpants. Meanwhile Dennis was busily occupied in removing his clothes as fast as he could, but he was not too busy to watch Betty and to be fascinated by her beautiful body.

Without a word, Betty took Dennis' hand and led him to the bed. "I've wanted you ever since I first walked into your office today," she breathed, between kisses.

"I'm afraid it took me a few minutes longer than that."

Dennis began kissing her shoulders, then her breasts, then the smooth, firm flesh of her abdomen. He sensed his arousal, and then felt the touch of Betty's soft fingers on his crotch.

They lay like that for several minutes, touching and kissing, and finally Betty whispered, "Turn over onto your back." Dennis obeyed, and she reached her leg over and straddled him. He entered her and they rocked back and forth, kissing each other deeply, with tongues highly active, Dennis' hands actively and alternately caressing her breasts and her buttocks.

Betty came to orgasm first, moaning softly, then slowing down her rocking movements. Dennis soon followed her, but continued kissing her body with his lips and tongue. Soon they separated and lay face to face, holding hands and nibbling each other's eyelids, noses, and lips.

A couple of hours later, Dennis arose from the bed. "I'm afraid I have to leave you for a while. I need to be at the midnight shift change. But I promise to be back in a short while."

Betty stirred in her sleep, and groaned softly. Dennis dressed quickly, turned the door handle slowly, opened the door, and reluctantly tiptoed out.

Early the next morning, Dennis awoke. Lying on her side and facing him, completely naked was Betty, who, when she saw he was awake, began to run her fingertips lightly across his chest, down his belly and onto his rapidly rising member.

This time Dennis climbed on top and began the process all over. When they were both satisfied, he said to her, "It's time for breakfast. Do we really need any?"

"Silly man, of course we do. And I'm treating you this time."

"You already have." Between pauses for kissing they slowly dressed and went out.

CHAPTER VIII

Ranger Jim Easton walked slowly down the beach. It was Monday morning after the big weekend, and he was expecting to see lots of trash left by all the RV people. He wasn't disappointed. The beach was littered with paper cups, plates, used disposable diapers, and other appetizing tidbits.

Easton reached down to his belt, pulled out his two-way radio and called park headquarters. "The beach is inundated with stuff; better send out a litter detail."

"Roger, we'll have one out there in about half an hour. Anything else to report?"

"Not so far. Easton out."

Jim continued his walk down the beach, internally reciting a well-practiced litany. *I keep wondering why people can't leave a place the way they found it. Even animals don't foul their own nests the way some of those beach campers leave their campsites.*
As for me, I've got to give up something. This business of working for the park, days, and lobstering at night has me wiped out. I'll have to talk to Doris. We just have to start cutting back, and learn to live on my salary. I'll lay it out for her tonight, before I go out in the boat.

Just then his reverie was interrupted as his attention was focused on a wooden dory floating just on the edge of the water. With each small wave that washed up on the beach the dory would advance and retreat, occasionally bouncing on the sand before slipping back in the tide.

Jim began to walk much more quickly towards the dory, and then began to run. He could just barely make out what seemed to be a human figure lying in the bottom of the dory. Then, as he neared the dory, he was sure it was a body.

Out again came the two-way radio. "Hello! Easton here. There's an old dory on the shore with what looks like a body in it. I'll try to grab it and pull it up on the beach."

"Okay, pull it up if you can, but don't touch anything. We'll try to get hold of the park superintendent. We'll be sending out a squad to take over, but stay where you are until you're relieved. Keep the area cleared."

Jim took off his work boots and socks and rolled up his pant legs above his knees. He waded into the surf and grabbed the painter of the dory and pulled it up on shore as far as he could, but the boat was very heavy. Jim could only get about a quarter of it up on the sand. By this time he was beginning to breathe quite rapidly. "Damn," he thought," I got my pants legs wet anyway!"

Looking into the boat, Jim could make out the body—and it certainly seemed to have no life in it—of a young man, clad in a white tee shirt, well bloodied around the chest area, a pair of well-worn jeans, no shoes or socks. Also lying in the bottom of the dory were a large flashlight, a pair of heavy duty orange rubber gloves, what looked like a manuscript enclosed in a plastic envelope, a box of heavy duty rubber bands, and a large, black handled fishing knife. There was a small engagement ring hanging on a rawhide lace around his neck.

Jim was mindful of his instructions not to touch anything, so, after his quick visual inspection, he concentrated on keeping away from the dory the small crowd which, by this time had gathered. Most of the people were occupants of the collection of RV's that were parked, scattered around, on the beach.

Jim, finally tired of trying to keep the crowd away, called out in a voice that carried authority, "Okay, folks, this is an emergency situation. Go back to your vehicles and get ready to leave this area, but wait there. Somebody will be around to ask you some questions. You'll have about ten minutes to vacate this beach after you've been questioned."

Gradually, accompanied by considerable grumbling, the crowd began to break up and, reluctantly wandered back to their trucks.

Just as the last of them moved away a Land Rover pulled up next to where Jim had pulled the boat, and four park rangers descended.

One of them, Stan Allridge, a deputy park superintendent, said to Easton, "Hi, Jim. Nice of you to provide us with some excitement. We haven't had any since yesterday."

"Okay, Stan. I haven't had time to see whether any of the RV people were witnesses to anything connected to this," said Jim.

"Thanks. We'll get a couple of our people on it right away. We've already made contact with the state police. They should be here any minute now. I guess they'll be taking this investigation over. The P'town police will need to be called also. We'll want a full report from you tonight. You'd better continue your patrol and keep an eye out for anything that might bear on this."

Jim left, thinking, *Wow! Wait 'til I tell Doris all about this. Wish I could stick around and see what happens.*

CHAPTER IX

Betty and Dennis were having breakfast in Bayside Betsy's, the same place where Diana and Bobby had eaten dinner the night before. Betty had just finished telling Dennis about her late husband. "He was a very dear man. I was only too happy to take care of him when the cancer made him dependent on me for most of his care. It broke my heart to see such a hale man deteriorate so rapidly. But, it's been a few years now since he passed away, and I'm getting back to living my life as a whole person again. And, thank goodness, he left me very comfortably off."

"I guess it must have been pretty rough on you, taking care of him for all that time, and then losing him."

"It was, but I'm all right now. You were starting to tell me more about yourself last night. What was the big mystery?"

"It's not really a mystery, although not a lot of people know about my life before I came back here to work."

"I'd be interested in hearing about it, if you are willing to tell me."

"Sure. When I left here after high school, and after four years in the army, I attended Harvard College. And after I graduated, I stayed on and qualified for my teaching license. I was full of great ideas of how I was going to revolutionize the field of education. I was going to be the savior of the kids in the inner city of Boston. I got a job teaching at an elementary school in Roxbury.

"After five years of knocking my head against the wall, trying to get some knowledge across to the kids, I realized that, if I had to act like a policeman, I might just as well become a real one. I wasn't doing them, or myself, any good. It got to the point that I felt sick at the thought of getting myself to school every day. I guess I just didn't have the guts it took to do that job. So I came back here and got a job as a cop."

"Wow! That's a side of you I wouldn't have guessed. I took you for a real tough guy." Only a second after those words came out of her mouth, Betty thought to herself, *Oh, God, how could I have said that? He'll think I'm putting him down, and that's not what I meant at all.*

"I guess I wasn't tough enough for *that* job."

Just then, an attractive young woman police officer wearing sergeant's stripes on her uniform entered the restaurant and approached the table where Betty and Dennis were sitting.

"Chief, can I talk to you, privately?"

Dennis rose and he and the sergeant walked to the front door. "What's happening?"

"We just got a call from the seashore park. They found a floater, only this floater wasn't in the water, he was in a boat."

"Have they made an identification?"

"No, they're waiting for the state police to arrive and take over, but they're not sure whether this is in their jurisdiction or ours. There's a stab wound on the victim's chest and it looks like it could be murder."

"Did they describe the victim?"

"Yeah, male, around middle twenties, dark hair, medium build and height. Sounds like it might be the young man we've been looking for."

"Okay, I'll get right back to my office. You'd better arrange to bring our homicide people into headquarters, and have Dot set up a meeting in my office in twenty minutes."

The sergeant, Janet Snow, left and Dennis walked slowly back to the table. Betty looked up to him and, seeing the concerned look on his face, said, "What's the matter? You look like you just lost your best friend."

"We have a tough case on our hands. I've got to get back to my office. Will you clear things up here?"

"Yes, of course. Will I see you later?"

"I'll leave a message for you at your B&B." Dennis walked out the door, wearing a very worried look.

CHAPTER X

B ack at the police station, Dennis looked around his office. There were three members of the detective squad arranged in a row opposite his desk. He reached for the pack of bubble gum and shoved a wad into his mouth. "Did Dot fill you in on what's happening with this missing man case?" he asked.

"Yeah, Chief, she did, and we also spoke to the officer-in-charge out at Race Point. It looks like there's a possibility that it's either the kid we were looking for or the one we picked up by mistake a couple of times." That was Sergeant Snow talking. She was usually the spokesman for the squad, which consisted of herself plus two uniformed officers temporarily assigned to the squad for the duration of the investigation.

"That's the damnable part of it. Probably, if that's true, the only person who could make a positive ID right now would be the Benton young man's mother. I sure hate to put her through that ordeal."

The three detectives sat back, fairly relaxed in their seats. They knew, with the state police, the park staff and the chief in the picture, they wouldn't be involved in any decision-making for some time to come, and the responsibility of involving the mother wouldn't be theirs. They knew it would have to be done and didn't envy Dennis his task. Word gets around a small, year-round community like Provincetown very quickly, and the whole department was aware of Dennis' relationship with Betty Benton by this time.

Dennis buzzed Dot on the intercom. " Please get me the head honcho at the Race Point station."

A few minutes later he picked up his phone handset and said,

"Hi, this is Chief Dawes. Can you fill me in on what's happening out there on that floater case?

"Uh huh, well I think we may be able to help you out on that," he continued in a moment. If it's one of two men we have been looking for, the mother of one of them can help you identify the victim. Yeah, I'll be willing to alert her; we have a sort of personal relationship. I think it might be easier for her to take if I tell her." Another pause. "I thought you'd feel that way. I'm sending three of my officers out there to work on the investigation. I'd appreciate your introducing them to the state cops who'll probably be arriving there soon."

Hanging up the phone, the chief turned to Snow and the others. "I guess you know what you have to do. They're expecting you at the Race Point Beach. If you need backup to keep the beach clear, let me know. I'm going to see Mrs. Benton and get her to try to identify the victim. God! At times like this, I wish somebody else was chief. And, Snow, remember, we want to stay friends with the state guys. Don't step on any toes while you're out there."

The three detectives rose and filed out the door; none of them was smiling.

Ten minutes later Dennis was at Betty Benton's rooming house and talking to Betty. "I'm going to ask you to get a tight grip on yourself, Betty, and do something really tough, but it's got to be done."

"It's Bobby, isn't it? I just knew something terrible was going to happen."

"Now take it easy; we don't know that anything has happened to Bobby. Someone has washed up on the beach, but at this point we don't have any identification. It would be a great help to us if you could rule Bobby out."

"It's okay, I couldn't stand not knowing. Have you spoken to Diana? She might know where Bobby is. Have you checked with that horrible professor? I'm sure he has something to do with this."

"We're checking everything out, Betty. Believe me, we're doing everything we can, right now."

They walked out to Dennis' patrol car and drove off, with the siren blaring and the lights flashing.

CHAPTER XI

A t the beach, Sgt. Snow and the other two detectives were talking to the medical examiner, who bent over the dory examining the victim. "Any idea yet what was the cause of death?" asked Snow.

"Ma'am, I shouldn't be telling you anything without permission from the state police, but it looks like he was stabbed in the heart, and that knife in the bottom of this boat might have been the weapon. We'll be doing the post as soon as we can get the body identified. Chief Dawes is on his way now with the woman who is supposed to make the ID."

A few minutes later Dennis came out onto the beach. He was supporting Betty, who was walking somewhat unsteadily, looking pale and breathing quite rapidly. They neared the group on the beach and Betty stopped suddenly. "I don't know if I can go through with this. Can't somebody else identify who it is and let me know?"

"I'm afraid you're going to have to be the one. I'll be right here with you." Dennis put his arm around her shoulder and helped her walk, or rather, almost stagger, over to the dory.

"Hi, Doc," Dennis said to the Medical Examiner. "This is Mrs. Benton. She may be related to the victim."

The doctor gently raised the edge of a short piece of canvas that was partially covering the body in the boat. Betty slowly and reluctantly looked down. "Oh, my God, it's Bill!" This time she did stagger, and Dennis caught her just as she was beginning to fall.

"Are you absolutely sure?"

A very weak "Yes" was her response. The doctor gently replaced the canvas and began to walk back to his vehicle. Noticing some tears coursing down Betty's cheek, Dennis handed her his handkerchief.

A few minutes later, Betty was beginning to recover from her shock and asked Dennis, "What happens now?"

"They'll be taking the body in for a post mortem exam, and they and we will start collecting evidence here and in town."

"I'm so relieved it wasn't Bobby but Bill is, *was* my nephew, and he has no living relatives that I know of. I guess Bobby and I will have to arrange for a funeral for him." After a couple of sobs, she murmured, "Poor Bill."

They watched as the medical examiner's assistants lifted the body out of the dory and onto a stretcher, which they carried across the beach and slid into the rear of the waiting station wagon.

Dennis helped Betty across the beach and into his cruiser, and they drove off, back to town.

CHAPTER XII

The detectives remained at the boat. Soon a state police cruiser arrived and three state troopers emerged. At least the detectives assumed they were troopers; none wore uniforms. After the introductions were made, Sergeant Snow asked the man in charge of the state police squad, a Sergeant Wallham, "How can we help without getting in you guys' way?"

"Well, as I see it, we could divide up forces to different jobs. This dory has to be turned over to the Coast Guard as soon as we're finished testing it. The testing should take us about two hours. After that we'd like you to take care of turning over the boat. Your group probably has some ideas about who might be involved in this. We'd appreciate a list of who should be checked out, and we can probably divvy it up between all of us. Also, a list of people you might check on with any murder, assuming this is one."

They all put on heavy latex gloves and grabbed the dory and hauled it up the beach so that it was completely out of the water. As the troopers began to work the dory over, Snow said, "I guess we'll leave you to work here. Call us at P'town headquarters when you want us to move the boat. Meantime we'll start on that list of names for you."

"Okay. Tell Chief Dawes we appreciate the help. Ask him whether he's still chewing that god-awful bubble gum. We'll call you as soon as we finish going over what's here."

Snow and the others walked back to their cruiser and drove off, and the state cops began working over the dory and its grisly contents.

Later, Betty Benton and Dennis were in Betty's room at the B&B talking. Betty was lying on the bed with a cold compress on her forehead. Dennis was seated in a small easy chair covered in a flowered chintz. Dennis looked extremely uncomfortable and ill at ease, as though he had had his body forced into that chair. Added to his physical discomfort was the strong scent emanating from a large bowl of potpourri placed on top of the dresser next to the bed. Both he and Betty were fully clothed.

"I still don't understand," said Betty wearily, " did they kill Bill purposely or did they mistake him for Bobby?" She shifted over on the bed to face Dennis, who was still wiggling to find a place for himself on that miserable chair, and not at all succeeding.

"That's what we're going to have to find out. The way I figure it, Bobby had only one person after him. This other guy, Bill, has quite a fishy smell about him (excuse the pun), and we don't have any definite clues about what he's mixed up in."

"If I weren't so upset about Bill, I'd probably find all this fascinating. Can you tell me what's going on now? And what you, yourself, will be doing?"

"The state police have pretty much taken over the investigation, and our job will be mostly to help with whatever they ask us to. Snow and her guys know what they need to do very well, so there isn't much for me to do except keep aware of what's happening and act as liaison with the state. Which reminds me, I'd better be getting back to the office right away."

"Oh, please don't go right now. Come and lie down next to me."

Dennis, somewhat gratefully, laboriously arose from that "hell chair" and lay down on the bed next to Betty. Within a short period of time, neither of them was fully clothed.

CHAPTER XIII

A fairly large group was assembled in Chief Dawes' office. Sergeant Wallham, who was the leader of the state police group, sat off to the right side of the chief's desk with his two men ranged behind him. On the left sat Sergeant Snow and her squad. "Why don't you tell us what you've come up with for a list," Dennis said to Snow.

Sergeant Snow reached into her inside jacket pocket and pulled out a small piece of paper. "It's a fairly short list so far. We're just getting started, and we're not too familiar with this cast of characters. We're pretty sure the victim was somehow involved in buying and distributing drugs here, although we don't have any specific evidence. If he was, then we have a few known creeps who would likely be involved, including the chief's favorite couple, Joe Stabile and Frank Barnes. Then there would be the crew that delivers the stuff, probably by boat, out in the bay."

At this point Sergeant Wallham interrupted. "I think you're on the right track there. We found some traces of cocaine in the dory."

"Good! That ought to help us narrow down our list somewhat. We also want to include Jack Brewer. He's been known to carry on a business other than taxi driving, or combined with it. His cab usually smells like funny cigarettes."

"Anyone else, like, maybe Al Saylor?" asked Dennis, "It's his dory."

"I was coming to him presently. And, we're not sure this had anything to do with the drugs. This guy looked a lot like the Benton kid. Maybe someone had it in for *him*. And, don't forget, we were looking for him before we found this body.

Sergeant Wallham spoke up again. "Who is this Benton kid? What does he have to do with Phillips?"

Dennis, very carefully choosing his words, spoke up from behind his desk. He sat hunched over, looking as though he was trying to hide, and very uncomfortable.

"He and Phillips were cousins. They were pretty much look-alikes, you know. We were told that Bobby Benton was believed to be here looking for his girl friend, and had a run-in with this professor of his who is staying out in one of the dune shacks, and…."

At this point Dennis ran out of breath and words, reached down for his trusty pack of bubble gum, shoved a piece in his mouth, chewed for a minute and began again. "He's gone again and we're looking for him. But, who knows, the professor might have been involved, thinking Phillips was Benton, and knocked off Phillips, or paid somebody to do it."

During this flood of words, Snow and her squad carefully avoided looking at Dennis, or each other, but sat there with unsuccessful attempts to keep grins off their faces.

Finally, after a long silence during which Dennis's face turned a dark red, Snow began again. "That pretty much covers our information. What have you gentlemen come up with?"

Sergeant Wallham pulled out a small notebook, opened it slowly, stared at it, and then addressed Dennis, "The medical examiner is sure now that the stab wound is the cause of death. We've examined the boat, and it's clean of fingerprints. There are no prints on the knife, but it looks like that's the weapon that the killer used. We think we can get some DNA from the rubber gloves or the flashlight we found in the boat."

He paused, looked again into the little book, and resumed. "From all our findings like the gloves, the knife and the rubber bands, it looks like the boat was also used to do some lobstering that night; probably from somebody else's traps."

For a while there was silence in the office, with the one exception the cracking of the chief's bubble gum. Then Sergeant Wallham looked around, saw no indication that anyone else wanted the floor, and said, "Okay, it looks like we ought to divvy up your list of possibles. Which ones do you want to handle?"

Dennis said, " We know Brewer, Barnes and Stabile and Al Saylor very well, so we can call them in. You might want to talk to Diana Wellman and Mrs. Benton to begin with. We can get together again in a couple of days, compare notes. I'd like to hit up the professor myself. How's that?"

"Fine, I'll be in touch." The three state detectives rose and exited.

CHAPTER XIV

The room was small and bare, with only a small table and two folding chairs, one on either side, and lit only by a gooseneck lamp on the table. Joe Stabile sat in one chair, Dennis Dawes in the other.

"All right, Joe, let's go over it again. The night of the Blessing of the Fleet. We know you and Frank rented a dory from Al Saylor, and he saw you rowing it out into the harbor at about nine o'clock. Start from there."

"Gosh, Chief, I don't know what this is all about! Me and Frank, we rented that old scow and went out and did some fishing out in the outer harbor. They wasn't biting so we rowed back in, tied up at Saylor's, and went home."

"Al says you didn't have any tackle in the boat when you took it out. How do you fish without tackle?"

"Why, we pulled into the beach near Frank's place and got some poles and supplies there and brought 'em back when we finished."

"The state detectives found traces of cocaine in the boat. Any idea how that could have got there? Al told us nobody had used that old boat since the last time it rained, so the coke couldn't have landed there before you guys had the boat."

"Cross my heart, Chief, we don't know nuthin' about that."

"We? How come you said 'we'? How would Frank know anything? He hasn't been told."

"Chief, you got me all mixed up. I didn't know what I was saying."

"Joe, it seems to me you have a choice. You can tell us about that cocaine and face a rap for drug smuggling, or keep quiet, and we'll probably charge you with murder. Now you can go back to your cell, and I'll be talking to your partner."

CHAPTER XV

Fifteen minutes later, Dennis was carrying on a similar conversation with Frank Barnes. "Frank, I'm not going to waste a lot of time talking to you. We know you weren't out there fishing, the night of the Blessing. We know you had something to do with bringing in the cocaine. We're pretty sure you were working with the murdered guy, Bill Phillips. Care to add anything?"

"Chief, I honestly don't know what you're talking about. Joe and I ain't had nuthin' to do with no cocaine."

"Okay, so you're as pure as the driven snow." Just then, Dennis realized his pun, unintentional as it was and groaned inwardly. "What do you know about Bill Phillips?"

Frank quickly drew in a breath, then hastily tried to cover it up with a fake cough. "I swear we had no part in that stabbing!"

"What stabbing? What makes you think he was stabbed?"

"Why, you said he was stabbed."

"No, I didn't say that at all. Okay, let's stop the games. Here's how we're gonna' work it: if you confess to you and Joe killing Phillips, and testify against Joe, we can probably get you a lighter sentence on the murder. But you'll have to serve additional time on the cocaine charge."

"You mean I should rat on my partner to get off on a murder rap we had nuthin' to do with?" Barnes began to sweat noticeably, began to wring his hands. He looked down at the table and sat there without speaking.

""We'll get you for that killing eventually. It'll go a lot easier for you if you confess. Just think, we could make the same offer to Joe. How long do you think he'll hold out before he comes our way?"

Dennis sat quietly for a minute or two, looking directly in Frank's face, chewing on his gum. Then he got out of his chair and opened the door and turned Frank over to a policeman standing outside the door.

He stood there, with his brow furrowed in deep thought for a few seconds, then said to himself, but aloud, "Well, at least now we know who did it. Now we need to find out why."

CHAPTER XVI

The next evening, Chief Dawes and Betty Benton were seated at a table in Ciro and Sal's restaurant on Commercial Street, with drinks before them, in anticipation of a sumptuous meal. Both had ordered minestrone and salad, and veal saltimbocca as their main dish, and Dennis had ordered a bottle of Chianti Classico.

Even before they were served, both were almost at the point of salivating heavily as the result of the heavenly aromas wafting about the restaurant. Dennis had explained that Ciro and Sal's was not too poor to have lampshades over the light bulbs, but that the food graters were in their place to provide atmosphere. As Dennis was catching Betty up on the latest events in the murder of Bill Phillips, Diana Wellman entered and, after looking around momentarily, walked over to their table, brushing past the hostess who was approaching her.

"If somebody doesn't tell me what's happened to Bobby now, I'll scream!" Diana announced.

"Get a chair and sit down, child." Betty didn't know whether to be annoyed at Diana for interrupting their private *tête-à-tête* or to be concerned, if Bobby was really missing again.

As soon as Diana sat down in the chair the waiter hurriedly brought up, she began again. "He's been staying with me in my motel, but he disappeared yesterday morning while I was showering, and I haven't heard from him since. Then, this morning that awful Professor Toro came to my motel and demanded to know where Bobby was. He said that Bobby had stolen the professor's manuscript. He was in a terrible snit and I'm afraid that, if he finds Bobby, he'll get violent."

"Do you have any idea where Bobby might be?" To himself, Dennis thought, "We really don't need this. I have enough on my plate at this moment: what looks like it's going to be a big drug case; the murder of that young man, and, now, Betty's son off on his own, somewhere."

He tried, somewhat unsuccessfully to adopt a casual or reassuring tone of voice and body language, but Betty thought, "I think Dennis is just as upset about Bobby as I'm getting."

Dennis excused himself, got up and walked out the door of the restaurant into the garden. He sat down on one of the benches placed there for the benefit of patrons who were forced to wait for a table, reached into his inside jacket pocket and brought out his cell phone. He dialed his office and said, "It's me. We have another missing case. Yeah, the same young man as last time. You have his description and identifying information. I'm in the middle of dinner, and I'll drop in the office when I'm finished." *Damn it!* That last to himself, silently, as he thought about what he might be missing later. He stood up and walked hesitantly back into the restaurant.

As he threaded his way between the tables to get to the women, Dennis heaved a great sigh, reached for his trusty bubble gum, then realized where he was and dropped his hand to his side.

"Did they find Bobby yet?" demanded Diana as soon as the chief was seated.

Dennis squelched the smartass response he was tempted to give Diana, mostly because Betty had guessed his intention, caught his eye, and slowly and discretely shook her head.

Dispensing with subtlety, Dennis turned to Diana and asked, "I guess you probably have had dinner already? There's a pretty good movie playing at the local theater. I can get one of my officers to walk you over to it, if you like."

"Thanks, but I haven't had dinner. I've been too upset."

"Oh, dear Diana, you must join us here."

Diana was ready to accept Betty's insincere invitation, then glanced at Dennis' facial expression, turned red and quickly rose and stammered an excuse and said, "I'm too tired and upset to eat.

I guess I'll see you at police headquarters tomorrow morning." Then she turned and fled.

Betty and Dennis ate a quiet and uncomfortable meal, relieved when it was over. Dennis paid the check, walked Betty back to her B&B in silence, pecked her on the cheek, and strode off angrily to his office.

CHAPTER XVII

Once in his office, Dennis put a call in to Sergeant Snow, who picked up her cell phone almost immediately.

"Sarge, we've got another complication in that murder case. Bobby Benton has disappeared again. I think we'd better have a talk with that professor of his, see what *his* involvement is in the whole schemozzle."

"Right, Chief, I'll drop by the professor's dune shack and, ahem, *invite* him in to headquarters for a little chat."

"Good! But don't come on too heavy with him. So far we have no evidence of his doing anything wrong."

"Don't worry, Chief, I'll be as smooth as silk."

"Okay, I'm going to my place, now. I'll see you in the morning."

"Your place? Okay, if I need anything I'll know where to find you." This last, from the good sergeant, was voiced in a somewhat incredulous tone of voice.

Dennis hung up his phone, swiveled his chair away from the desk, and began to wonder. "Was I being a stupid idiot back there at Ciro's? I'm sure Betty thought I was acting like one. Well, it's been quite a while since I screwed up in a relationship with a nice woman." Acting on a sudden hunch, Dennis picked up the phone and called Betty's bed and breakfast. He asked for Betty, and when she said hello, he was unable to say anything for a long second, then suddenly inspired, said, "Hi."

"Yes?" was her icy response after identifying Dennis.

"Look, Betty, I realize that I acted like a damn fool earlier. It's just that that dizzy dame got my temper up. I was upset that she was spoiling our whole evening, so I kinda' lost control. I apologize to you, and I will to Diane, if that will help."

"I'm not sure that will help. I think maybe you're carrying on too many roles in all this, and you're having trouble making all those roles work properly."

"Whoa! Say that again in my language! I'm not sure I follow you. Do you mean that we shouldn't have a relationship because of what's happening with your son and your nephew?"

"I think that's it, basically. I'm willing to get together to talk tomorrow. Right now I'm too upset and confused. Good night!" and she hung up.

Dennis slammed his phone down, uttered several well-chosen expletives and grabbed for his bubble gum.

CHAPTER XVIII

The next morning the chief was seated at his desk, chewing away mightily at his bubble gum, and swiveled around to face his "guest," Professor Toro. "Professor, what can you tell us about your activities on the day of the fleet blessing, and, particularly, during that evening and night?"

"Chief, I don't like being dragged in here like a common criminal. I don't know why you are doing this. Are you charging me with some crime? Until you tell me what's going on, I refuse to answer any of your questions."

"I'd be delighted! We have a murder that was committed here in P'town that night; a drug smuggling case connected to that in some way; the victim closely resembled a man you've had a stormy relationship with, to say the least; and now that same young man is missing again. Now, would you like to answer a few questions or shall we arrest you on charges of littering the beach and hold you for questioning?"

"Well, if you put it that way, I'll be happy to assist the police in any way that I can. What can I tell you?"

"Start with the afternoon of the Blessing. Just retrace your steps from then until the next morning. Where were you, what did you do, who were you with? All that."

"Well, that afternoon Miss Wellman and I were at my little place, preparing to get to work on a project I'm developing, when one of my students, a Robert Benton, burst in and disturbed us, and finally went off with Diana. I continued to arrange my materials, did some writing, then fixed dinner and ate it all alone, and finally went to bed."

"Sorry to interrupt you, but how do you get around here?"

"I've rented a Jeep."

"Do you happen to know the license plate number?"

"Yes. It's Massachusetts number L69324. Why are you asking?"

"One of my men saw a green Jeep with that number illegally parked in front of Saylor's Boat Yard at about ten o'clock that night. He didn't ticket it, but he did report it. Any ideas about how that could have happened, if, as you say, you were at your shack all evening?"

"Oh, that's right. I drove into town to get a pack of cigarettes."

"Do you usually smoke? It's not a good idea out in those shacks."

" I was feeling upset about that confrontation, so I thought a cigarette would calm my nerves."

"Did anybody see you? Where did you buy the cigarettes? How long were you in town? What else did you do beside buy the smokes?"

"Now, which question do you want me to answer first? The stores were all closed, so I didn't buy any cigarettes. I didn't buy anything, just got back in the Jeep and rode back to the house. Now, are you going to tell me what this is all about? I'm not without important friends back in Boston, you know, and I'm not used to being treated like this."

"Like what, Professor? We have a serious couple of cases going on here right now, and, one way or another, you're involved, so though I'm delighted that you have important friends, you're still going to answer any questions I have, either from in or out of jail!"

"I think I have no more to say."

Dennis got up, walked to the door, opened it and called to one of the officers outside. "Charley, book this gentlemen on a charge of illegal parking, scofflawing, and creating a public nuisance. Then let him call his lawyer."

"Look, Chief, let's discuss this reasonably. What is it you really want to know that I can tell you? I don't think you'll get anywhere in your investigation by harassing me."

"Right! We are in the middle of investigating, not only this murder, but the likelihood of a big drug delivery that was probably taking place right at or near where your car was parked the night of the fleet blessing. We're about to call in the Feds on that one. Now would you like to tell me about why you lied to me at first, and what you really were doing at Saylor's Boat Yard at ten o'clock that night, and what's your connection to William Phillips?"

"All right. First of all, I had some business to transact, some business with William Phillips. We had a date to meet at Saylor's at ten that night. I knew he and Robert Benton were cousins and had been friends at school a few years ago. I wanted him to coax Benton to work more cooperatively with me on the article we were cowriting."

"Why would he do that for you? Phillips, I mean."

"When he was at BU, he got into some trouble. He was accused of date raping a female student. I convinced her not to bring charges, and he has been grateful to me ever since. Every once in a while I ask him to do me some favor or another."

"I don't think I want to know what some of those favors were! Did you meet with Phillips that night?"

"No, he never showed up. But I did meet up with a couple of very unpleasant looking men who were just coming ashore in an old wooden boat. They looked at me like I had offended them in some way. One of them was carrying a package that seemed to be rather heavy. They opened the door to the yard office, which was lighted, went in, and came out a few minutes later without the package. They didn't speak, and just then, an old beaten-up taxi parked in front of the yard and they both got in, and the taxi drove away."

"When they were in the office, could you hear anything?"

"Just the muffled sounds of people talking. I couldn't make out any of the words. The sounds of their voices were very quiet at first and then became quite loud just before the two came out."

"Anybody else show up?"

"No. At that time I began to feel quite tired, so I returned to my place and retired for the night."

"If necessary, could you identify the two men you saw?"

"I think so. It was quite dark, but I think I can."

"I'm going to let you go. Don't discuss what you've told me with anyone else, except other cops. Don't leave town. We'll be keeping an eye on you. Okay, you can leave."

Professor Toro stood up, cast an indignant look at Dennis, and strode out of the office without another word.

CHAPTER XVIV

J ack, we've known each other for a long time. I find it hard to believe that you're mixed up in this murder, but you've been seen with this Phillips guy lots of places around town." Dennis was addressing this to Jack Brewer, whom the detectives had brought in to Provincetown Police headquarters.

"Not only that, but you were seen picking up Stabile and Barnes the night of the murder, and, God knows, those two guys are involved up their ears. So, talk to me."

"What can I tell you, Chief? I took those guys to Joe's house, waited for them a while, then took them back to Saylor's and left them there. So help me, that's all I know."

"Sure you're not forgetting anything? They say anything about what was going on? Anything you can tell me?"

"Well, the only thing I noticed was that they were wearing different clothes when I took them back."

"Different? How different?"

"They both was wearing different shirts, and I think they had changed their jeans, but it's hard to tell one pair of filthy jeans from another. My cab smelled from whiskey on the way back to the boat yard. Took me a couple of days to get rid of the stink. And those two guys were staggering a little bit when they got out."

"What did you do after you dropped them off?"

"I drove home and went to bed."

"Any witnesses to when you got home?"

"Yeah, my wife was waiting for me, to give me hell for being out that late. She was sure I was with another woman."

"I'll be talking to her. Now, let's talk about you and the late Bill Phillips. I've been warning you for a long time to stay away from the funny business. Now it's getting a lot more serious. There was a big delivery going on that night, we're damn sure, and it's probably tied to the murder, and anybody connected with the drugs will be spending some vacation time with Uncle Sam. Okay, you can get out."

After Brewer had left, Dennis sat at his desk, his mind churning with almost random thoughts about the murder; about the drug delivery; finally, about his relationship with Betty Benton.

I don't think I want to put off that conversation any longer, Dennis said to himself as he reached for the phone.

A few minutes after, he and Betty were seated at a secluded table in Sally's Cafe on Commercial Street. Betty was the first to speak after they ordered coffee and doughnuts. "I've been doing a lot of thinking about us. First of all, is there an us?"

"Depends on what you mean by 'an us'. If you want to talk about specific outcomes right now, I don't think—what with everything that's going on—I'm ready for that."

"I wasn't thinking that far ahead, but I would like to know whether our personal relationship is more than just a couple of rolls in the hay. Or is it something more than that?"

"Betty, I would hope you'd know that it's a lot more than that for me. I'm not growing any younger. I haven't had many serious relationships with women in a long while. I'm serious about this one, but I need some space while we're getting to know one another. How does that sit with you?"

"I've had the feeling all along that you're sort of hanging back, not wanting to get too involved. I thought at first that would be enough for me. Now I'm not so sure. And I believe that what's been happening, Bobby's disappearances and Bill's murder, have been affecting our relationship, since they're part of your professional responsibilities."

"Betty, I want you to know that I really like you a lot. Maybe, after all this business is over we'll be able to straighten things out. I think it might be best for you to go back to Boston for now. I'd be willing to bet that Bobby will show up when he's ready, and we'll certainly let you know as soon as he surfaces."

Betty noticed that Dennis' hand was shaking as he raised his coffee mug up to his lips, something she hadn't seen him do before, and at the same time she realized she, herself was on the verge of tears.

"Give me your Boston phone number. I'll call you in a couple of days. I don't know what to say."

"Maybe *goodbye* would be the most honest thing to say."

Without a word, Dennis dropped a ten-dollar-bill on the table, got up and walked out, without a backward glance.

Betty sat still for a moment, tears flooding her cheeks. Then she dropped her head on her arms on the table, and wept silently.

CHAPTER XX

When Dennis returned to headquarters, Dot stopped him before he entered his office and whispered, "The state police detectives are in there waiting for you. They didn't sound too friendly. You can still leave without their seeing you."

"Thanks, but I'll talk to them now." He entered his office. "Hi, guys."

Sergeant Wallham and two of his men were seated in front of his desk, rather rigid in their chairs, and looking stonily at him.

As Dennis sat down Sergeant Wallham began. "Dennis, we thought this was going to be a cooperative venture. It's come to our attention that you've been busy interviewing lots of characters here, but we haven't heard a word from you in days. Would you like to bring us up to date? We are supposed to be in charge of this investigation, you know."

"I'm sorry, I've had a lot on my mind lately, and most of it doesn't belong to this investigation, and I apologize for not keeping you abreast."

Dennis then rapidly filled in the state detectives on the results of his interviews. The three detectives took notes as Dennis talked. Gradually the angry looks eased on their faces, and the atmosphere became more relaxed.

"Sounds like a nice, long list of people who might have done it. Are there any more we still don't know about?"

After a slight pause, Dennis smiled a wry smile and sighed. "There's at least one more possibility. Jim Easton, the park ranger who discovered the body in the boat, is connected somehow with the professor, and I think that relationship bears looking into."

"We've been doing some checking at the university, and that professor doesn't come out smelling like a rose. From what we've learned, his status there is very tenuous, and he needs to get hold of the work that the young Benton is writing up. Do you suppose he killed Phillips, thinking it was Benton, to get the paper?"

"I certainly wouldn't rule it out. I've been mulling over an idea. Maybe we ought to chart out a chronology and list all the events and actions and locations of people we know about for sure. That way, I think we can get a perception of all the things that went on that day and night."

"Good idea! Why don't we get started on it right now?"

The group moved from Dennis' office to a conference room with a large table and about a dozen chairs arranged around it. At Dennis' phoned instruction, Dot called Sergeant Snow, and she and her men also moved into the conference room. Two hours later Dennis phoned Dot again and ordered lunch to be brought in for the group, as well as a pack of bubble gum for himself.

Policemen wandering in and out of the building were warned by Dot and kept their conversations low-keyed and opened and shut doors and drawers quietly.

CHAPTER XXI

L ate that afternoon, Sergeant Wallham, who by this time had taken charge of the group, raised his head and looked around the table. "I think we ought to stop here and see what we've got. George, let's hear what you've been recording so far."

The trooper began. "We start with that Sunday afternoon. Ms. Benton visited Chief Dawes in his office to report her son missing. After she left, she engaged Jack Brewer to drive her to Professor Toro's shack to look for her son Robert Benton there. She did not find her son, or anyone else for that matter, there. She and Brewer left, and we know that she rented a room at the Seaside Bed and Breakfast. She had dinner with the chief, and they spent...well, she's accounted for.

"Witnesses locate Brewer meeting with the victim William Phillips in John's Cafe shortly after Brewer returned from the Professor's. They were there for about half an hour, and Brewer drove his cab to McMillan Wharf and remained there for several hours looking for fares.

"We've lost track of Phillips until about nine o'clock that night, when he was seen entering the office at Saylor's Boat Yard. He wasn't seen after that until his body was discovered in the dory.

"The chief here confronted the two men, Stabile and Barnes, in the afternoon. They were seen by several police officers wandering around Commercial Street, not doing anything suspicious. They were seen to be accosted on the street by a man later identified as Professor Toro, held a long conversation, and then, at about seven p.m. were at Saylor's Boat Yard, rented the dory, and rowed out into the harbor. At about ten that night, they were reportedly seen at the boat yard by Professor Toro, were picked up by Brewer's taxi and returned, dressed in different clothing, a little while later."

At this point, George hesitated, looked around the table and asked whether there were any questions or corrections about what he had read. Receiving no response, he continued.

"Professor Truro was at his shack with Ms. Wellman in the afternoon working on a project, when they were interrupted by Robert Benton. A somewhat stormy confrontation then followed, then Benton and Wellman left. We don't know what the Prof did until he relates that he drove into town that evening at around ten, but we do know that he was not at his shack when Ms. Benton and Brewer came by in mid afternoon.

"Ms. Wellman claims that she and Benton returned to her motel and he left her there, where she remained for the rest of that night. The next morning she says he called her and they met at breakfast in town and spent the rest of the day together acting like tourists. We have no knowledge of where and how Robert Benton spent that night. Ms. Wellman might be able to tell us.

"We can locate Jack Brewer at the boat yard twice that night. At about ten or ten-thirty, he was seen, or rather his taxi was seen, at Macmillan Wharf periodically during the night, apparently looking for fares.

"Jim Easton, the park ranger was at work all day until about six when, according to Ms. Easton, he returned home and ate dinner. He went out on his lobster boat, they say, and returned at about eleven o'clock and spent the rest of the night at home with her. They had no visitors to substantiate any of this. No one saw him go out in his boat. Or come back in."

Again George stopped and looked around the room. "That seems to be all the definite information we have at this time."

"I think that was a very accurate summation of what we have, George. Thank you very much. For everyone's information, I spoke to the medical examiner before I came here, and he now estimates the time of death at somewhere between nine-thirty and eleven that night."

Wallham again glanced around. "I think we've accomplished all we can this afternoon. I'd like to have us all digest what we have and see who comes up with any ideas. Let's meet again here at eight o'clock tomorrow morning. Okay, Dennis?"

"Sure. We'll have 'coffee and' ready and waiting."

CHAPTER XXII

It was late on that bright, sunny and windless afternoon on Coast Guard Beach in Eastham, and Bobby Benton, clad only in a pair of cutoff jeans and a baseball cap marked with a red capital B, was working with a small shovel and an assortment of brushes. Some of them resembled artists' brushes and some those of house painters. He had just shoveled off a very thin layer of sand from a small area of beach and was gently brushing what remained of the sand from what looked like the edge of a pit.

He was approached by an older man who was dressed in khakis and work boots and wearing a tropical helmet. "Bobby, are you at a point where you can stop, just now? I need to talk to you."

Bobby stopped his brushing, laid down his brush, and straightened up and said, "Shoot, Dr. Lynn. What's it about?"

"I was just reading a copy of the Cape Cod Times, and there was an article in there about a murder in Provincetown and it mentioned in passing that you were involved in some way, and that you were missing. Care to tell me about that?"

"Damn it! I can't seem to get away from that mess! I'm sorry, Dr. Lynn, I was afraid you wouldn't hire me if you thought I was involved. It was a distant cousin of mine who was murdered, and they think that maybe he was mistaken for me."

"Look, son, I don't want to go mixing in your business, but don't you think people down there in P'town are worrying about you? Would it interfere with your plans if you at least let them know you're alive?"

"I'm sure the police would want to question me. And they might even arrest me on suspicion of murder. Bill, my cousin, had a ring that belonged to me, and I made some threats about getting it back from him. I know my mom's worrying, but hopefully they'll catch whoever did it and I can stay here and work with you and finish my study."

"I have an idea. Suppose I was willing to guarantee that you wouldn't take off, would you be willing to call the police and tell them that you are safe here, and would make yourself available if they need you?"

"I suppose that could work out okay. Can I use your cell phone, please?"

"Sure, son, go ahead. But I think you might stop brushing where you were. That pit has been discovered six or seven times by student interns before you."

"Provincetown Police Department, Officer Sears speaking."

"Officer, my name is Robert Benton. I'd like to speak with Chief Dawes."

"Just a minute, sir, I'll connect you."

Bobby waited for a minute. "This is Chief Dawes, Bobby. I won't mince words with you. Call your mother, then get your ass down here pronto."

"Chief, my sponsor here would like a word with you. Chief, this is Dr. Henry Lynn, of the Archaeology Department of Brookline University."

"Hello. Chief Dawes. I'm in charge of the dig here at Coast Guard Beach. We're just finishing up with this one section and will be closing down for the season in about three or four days. If we could keep Bobby here 'til then, it would be a big help, and I'd be willing to have him under my recognizance."

"All right, but I'll need a statement from you expressing that in writing. And, on an official letterhead. And tell that lunkhead to call his mother."

CHAPTER XXIII

The chief banged his telephone down, sat in his seat for a minute chomping heavily on his bubble gum, and pondering his next move.

"Is that kid really going to call his mother? Maybe I'd better call her. If I do, will she talk to me? Maybe this time I'll be able to open my big mouth and tell her how I really feel. Yeah, but will she listen?"

Three more chews and he reached his decision. He picked up his phone again and asked Dot to put his call through to Betty, of course referring to her as Ms. Benton.

When Betty picked up the phone, "Hello, Betty, this is Dennis. Did you just hear from Bobby?"

"Yes, and I'm so relieved! He told me that twice you told him to call me. I thank you for that. Was there anything else?"

"Yes, there is. The last few days, I've been thinking of you a lot. And I miss you a lot. Would it be possible for you to come down here this weekend, so we can talk without any pressure? I don't want our relationship to just end."

"I'm sorry, but I have a date for this weekend. Perhaps we could make it for some other time?"

"Well, if you're dating somebody, it doesn't make too much sense for you to come down here."

"I didn't say I was dating someone else. I just have a date for Saturday night."

"Does that mean you'd be willing to come next week end?"

"I guess so, that is, if you really want me to. "

"No, it's got to be on both our heads. We both need to take responsibility for where we're going."

"You're right. Okay, I'll be there on Friday on the one o'clock boat. Will you meet me there?"

"Yes, I'll be there. In case of an emergency, I'll have one of my men meet you there. Do you want the same B&B as last time?"

After a long pause, "No, why don't we wait until I get there and see how things go?"

"Fine, see you on Friday at the one o'clock boat." As he hung up Dennis was wondering, "Now what in hell does she mean by that?"

CHAPTER XXIV

At eight the next morning, all the detectives were assembled again in the conference room, along with Dennis, Sergeant Snow and Sergeant Wallham. Again, Sergeant Wallham took the lead.

"Here's what else we've got. The M.E. tells us that the stab wound was the cause of death. The lab has checked the knife, and all the other objects found in the dory for fingerprints. The handle of the knife, which they say was the one used by the killer to stab Phillips, was too rough to hold any prints.

"We've been getting DNA samples from as many of the suspects as possible. Stabile and Barnes's from their coffee cups here at the jail, Brewer's from some of the hundreds of cigarette butts in his taxi, Ms. Benton's we got from...." Here the sergeant broke off, looked at Dennis's eyes quizzically, and, seeing no answer there said, "Well, anyway we got some."

"We still need to get samples from Robert Benton, Professor Toro, Ms. Wellman, Jim Easton and Al Saylor. There were no traces of the dead man's DNA in any part of the dory, except where he was lying. To us that means he was probably dead before he was placed in the dory."

One of Sergeant Snow's men raised his hands, as though he were in class. Wallham gave him a go-ahead glance and the officer asked, "How come you get these samples on the sly? Can't you just take them from the suspects?"

The sergeant patiently responded. "To do that we need to get a court order, then the suspects can stonewall us for a while. We do face a problem of secure identification and admissibility in court at a subsequent trial, though. But then we can easily get a court order at that time."

Dennis couldn't hold back any longer. "Were you able to make any positive idents on anything on the boat or on the body?"

"Yes, we got some DNA samples of both Stabile and Barnes on the oar handles, also some of theirs on parts of the body. We were able to get the clothes the two were wearing. The shirts had traces of human blood of the same type as the victim's. There were also minute traces of the fibers of their shirts on the clothing on the body.

"The way we put it together, the two of them loaded the body in the boat, rowed it out past the end of Long Point and left it to drift, and were picked up by someone in another boat, or were towing it from another boat. They obviously hoped the dory would drift out to sea on the outgoing tide. In the condition it was in, it probably would have sunk fairly soon, but it was a stupid way to dispose of a body."

"That points it more clearly at those two." This from Sergeant Snow. "Why don't we book 'em on a murder charge, Chief?"

"We don't know for sure that they committed the murder. They could have been hired by the killer to dispose of the victim, and did their usual screw-up."

Sergeant Wallham nodded. "So far we can't prove that both of them or even one of them killed Phillips. We still have a good deal of work to do before anyone is charged with the murder. Chief, can you arrange to get us samples of DNA from young Benton, and Ms. Wellman? We've tried to get samples of the professor's from his used dishes when he goes out, but he locks the whole place up so tight that we can't get in without breaking in."

"Do we have enough on him to warrant getting a court order for his DNA?" asked Dennis.

"Probably. He admits to being right outside where the murder likely took place. We found traces of blood matching the victim's type in the boat yard office.

"I think that brings us up-to-date. Do you want to add anything now, Dennis?"

"No, I guess you've covered everything. Meet tomorrow morning?"

"Yeah, and this time we'll bring the doughnuts."

"In the meantime, I'll talk to our two 'guests' and see what else we can get out of them."

CHAPTER XXV

This time Sergeant Snow accompanied Dennis as he questioned Joe Stabile. "Joe, we've got an awful lot on you. We can easily connect you and Frank with trying to dispose of Phillips's body in the dory. We have DNA evidence that both of you handled the body. We won't need much more evidence to be able to charge you with Murder One. If you didn't actually commit the killing, you must know who did. So make it easy on yourself. Talk to me!"

"Chief, I'm not going to say anything."

Dennis sent the man back to his cell and asked to have Frank Barnes brought in to the interviewing room.

"Frank, you're in real deep shit. It won't take more than another day or so 'til we have the goods on you for at least Murder Two, and most likely, Murder One. And right now we've got you dead to rights on quite a few drug charges. I can't promise you anything, but I would guess that if you come clean we might be able to get the DA to do some bargaining."

Silence from Frank.

"Don't forget, there are two of you involved, and whichever one of you helps us out, things'll go easier for him. Don't answer me right now. Take a couple of hours to think it over. I'll talk to you again later."

The chief turned Frank Barnes over to an officer, after a whispered conversation that Frank could not overhear: "Make sure that those two are kept very separate, and have no chance to talk to each other. We'll let them sweat for awhile."

When the two police officers were alone, Snow, obviously frustrated, said to Dennis, "Why are you going so easy on those two? We ought to be getting real rough with them. Leave me and one of my men alone with them, one at a time, and we'll soon get them talking!"

Dennis responded, "Did you ever hear of what's called the Prisoner's Dilemma Game?"

"No, what's that?"

"It's a hypothetical situation where two guys commit a crime and get arrested and put in jail. The sheriff puts them in separate cells and tells them, separately, that whichever one confesses and incriminates the other will get off with a light sentence, while they'll throw the book at the other. So each one has to decide among several outcomes. If they both keep quiet, they will probably go to prison on a lesser charge; to be successful at that, they each have to trust the other guy.

"But, since they can't communicate with each other, possibly one, or both, thinking the other guy will turn state's evidence, would be likely choose to be the first to squeal."

"I don't see where the game comes in."

"People who teach what's called Conflict Resolution use the game to demonstrate the way conflicts can be resolved using a win-win approach. Generally, the way the game turns out, one or both of the criminals talks, and they both lose."

"So, what are you expecting these creeps to do?"

"I think they're not smart enough or trusting of each other enough to keep quiet and end up with only a drug charge. Maybe it'll get at least one of them worried enough to do some talking."

"So where did you learn about that game?"

"I learned it at the Ed School at Harvard and, when I was teaching in Boston, I used to use it with the kids to solve, let's say, interpersonal difficulties."

"And it worked?"

"I'm talking about problem solving. Sometimes it worked. It even got to the point where kids would use the technique when some other kids were working up to a fight."

"Well, I wish you luck in this case. But, if it doesn't work, we can question them with a little bit of muscle."

"Thanks, but hopefully my approach will work."

CHAPTER XXVI

C hief, there's a call for you on line one. I think it's Ms. Benton."

"Thanks, Dot. Hello, this is Dennis. Betty?"

"Dennis, I'm sorry to bother you, but I think we shouldn't wait for two weeks to get together. I can get a cruise boat down there tomorrow morning and be there about noon. Would you be able to take some time off so we can talk?"

"I think that's a real good idea, Betty. We need to get things straight. I'll meet you at the wharf."

"Until tomorrow, then. Bye."

"See you."

On Friday, the sun was shining brightly, with no clouds to break up a continuously clear blue sky. As the dockhands nonchalantly eased the docking lines from the bollards on the dock the steamer slipped quietly away from its berth and moved out into Boston Harbor.

Betty stood at the rail and watched, fascinated—almost to the extent of being hypnotized—by the small bow wave generated by the ship as it spread diagonally over the water on both sides. Reflections from the sun off the gently rippling water created millions of diamonds glittering off the surface of the harbor. Slowly, the steamer passed the many harbor islands, some islands full of trippers from the city for a day's recreation. The ship made its turn out into Massachusetts Bay and surged ahead, picking up speed.

On deck, and spread throughout the ship, hundreds of passengers occupied themselves in a variety of fashions. Casual attire seemed to be the rule of the day, with most men clad in shorts and tee shirts or polo shirts. Most women were similarly attired; the variety of self-expression seemed to be only in the area of footwear. No two people on board appeared to have wanted to wear the same shoes, sandals, slippers, swim soccer, in more than a few instances, bare feet. Groups of children, seemingly ranging in ages from about eight or ten to about fifteen or sixteen ran from place to place, or slowly moved in couples from one vantage point to another.

Looking at them, with their pant bottoms wrapped around their ankles or dragging a good part of their length on the deck and parts of their rumps exposed above the pants, Betty thought to herself, "I'm sure glad Bobby doesn't dress like that." At least, Betty thought, none of the kids was asking his or her parents, "When will we be getting there?"

Many of the parents, meanwhile, were sitting in deck chairs in couples or groups, chatting, exchanging plans they had made for the day in P'town, or boasting of the vacations they would begin as soon as the boat reached the Cape. Everyone looked relaxed, at ease, and quietly anticipating what the day might present.

This was not so for Betty. Over and over in her mind she kept asking herself, *Why am I doing this? I thought we had resolved the questions about our affair, and where it was going. Nowhere, that's where I felt it was going. Affair! Is that what it is? I know that I wouldn't be satisfied with just that.*

And what about Dennis? He sounded as though he wanted more also, but, as a communicator he was no great shakes, so it was pretty hard to guess what he was thinking or feeling. Well, I'm not going to come up with any answers until Dennis and I get together, and even then, he may not be willing or able to be open with me. I may have to be more direct, or directive, to get things going.

She continued to stare out at the water. Then, as the steamer began to round Wood End, the tip of Cape Cod, she began getting her things in order.

At noon Dennis was waiting impatiently on the wharf for the Boston boat to arrive. Sure enough, it rounded Wood End and steamed into the dock. After a few minutes the crew set the boat's docking lines and arranged the gangplank. The horde of passengers, set for a day of swimming, biking, shopping, and just sightseeing, began tramping onto the dock. A few minutes later, Dennis was able to spot Betty coming down the gangplank and trying to avoid being trampled in the rush.

As soon as her feet touched the dock Dennis moved quickly to where Betty was standing and took her hand. Then, seeing an okay in her eyes, he grabbed her in a tight hug, and she returned it.

"Okay, Dennis, I need to breathe now."

"Have you had lunch? We can go to Napi's if you like."

"No, thanks but I want to go someplace where we can talk and not be interrupted or overheard."

"Well, we can drive over to Race Point Visitor Center and just sit in my car and talk."

"You know, I've never seen your house. Why don't we go there, and we can fix us some lunch, and have our talk?"

"Well, if you promise not to look at this morning's dirty dishes in the sink, and a few dirty clothes lying on the bathroom floor, I guess we can. Are you sure you want to go there?"

"Fine with me if it's all right with you. We don't want your neighbors gossiping about the two of us."

"What I do in my own home is my own damned business! Let's go!"

The two got into the chief's cruiser and drove off the wharf and into town. Dennis parked his vehicle in back of the police department and they walked over to Bradford Street, turned left and proceeded a couple of blocks. They turned right and entered the front walk of a small, typical Cape Cod house. Behind a low, white picket fence was a neat, well-tended flower garden. Betty slowed her steps as she admired the pretty flowers blooming in profusion, then they entered the house.

Betty found the interior to be quite different from what she had imagined it to be. The living room, entered from the warmly colored and decorated front hallway was furnished in a nautical style. There were several oil paintings hung on the walls, mostly of seascapes or of sailing vessels traveling through rough seas. On the mantle was a ship's clock. Next to it, mounted on a board, was a sailboat half model. Off in a corner on the mantle was a highly varnished block of wood, which looked to be mahogany, and near the top a Band-Aid was embedded under the varnish. Below the bandage was printed in black letters: "VALIANT CREW"

"What is that?" Asked Betty, pointing.

Dennis was delighted to have something not personal to talk about. "Something pretty silly from a long time ago. If you are interested, I can tell you in about ten minutes."

"I think I would love to hear it if it's about you."

"Okay. Quite a few years ago, I used to sailboat race as crew for a good friend of mine. This guy owned a boatyard, and he was a dealer for the class of boats we used to race, so his boat had every gadget you can imagine. He was great at starting, was usually the first boat across the start line.

"The trouble was, he ran the boat like a democracy, always taking polls on every decision. So we'd get to the first mark, usually upwind in first place, then would come the first poll: "Guys, should we put up the spinnaker?" By the time we reached that decision, we were usually last. That pattern lasted for several years. Then one year, we added another crew member who had just sold his racing boat to buy a cruising sailboat.

"This guy, call him Roger, was only used to winning, and before you knew it, we were spending three or four afternoons a week practicing: practicing getting the spinnaker up and down, practicing gybing the spinnaker from one course to the other. We practiced just about anything that could cut a few seconds off our time. I was assigned the job of foredeck crew, which meant my being at the forward end of the cockpit, reaching forward to shift either the jib or spinnaker from one side of the boat to the other, then setting it in the right position. To do that I had to grab the hardware that hung from the clew of the sail and it was mostly held together by shackles and cotter pins, so I ended up every Saturday afternoon spilling copious amounts of blood from my hands. At the end of the racing season, my friend gave me a bottle of very expensive red wine to make up for the blood, and that plaque."

"And did you begin to win races?"

"Well, we won the cup for the Fourth of July Regatta, but only one or two races after that. And by the next year, I didn't want to spend the time, so I quit crewing for my friend."

"Did it bother you to give up sailing?"

"In the first place, I was never that caught up in racing, and I certainly never got so excited about winning, like lots of racing skippers. I preferred to day sail or cruise on my own boat when I was able to buy one, so I never really missed racing. Besides, the harbor where I originally kept my boat used to have pickup races whenever enough guys got together, and the races were usually for who was going to buy the beer that night. I can tell you, I've bought more than my share of the beer. End of story."

A couple of straight-backed armchairs stood either side of a round antique three-legged table. The coffee table was an old ship's hatch cover, which Dennis had taken down to the bare wood and refinished in a light reddish brown. On the table stood a brass pot containing a green ivy plant, a block from an old sailing ship, as well as a few, relatively unread, coffee table art books.

A couple of straight upholstered love seats and comfortable chairs with their attendant end tables completed the furniture. The wide planked floor, stained a dark brown, was partially covered by a large oval braided rug.

"Wow! I'm really impressed. I never expected anything like this."

"Well, I have to live someplace."

"No, what I meant was this place looks like it was done by a decorator, not a man who lives alone."

"To tell the truth, I had help from a live-in girl friend who was a decorator. That was a couple of years back, but I like the marine touch. It's almost like being on my boat when I come in here."

"I didn't know you were a sailor. Tell me about your boat."

"Oh, you'll love her. She's a sloop, twenty-eight feet, overall.

She has a cabin with a fully equipped galley and carries enough sail to make up to about eight knots in a good breeze. I have her rigged so I can single-hand her, but two people are very comfortable in the cockpit. And below, also. As soon as this case is over with, I'd like to take you out, maybe weekend down to Plymouth or Sandwich, maybe." This last 'maybe' was spoken in a hesitant, questioning tone.

"I think before we talk about sailing, we have more immediate matters to talk about. I'm still not sure what you have in mind as far as our relationship is concerned. You were just mentioning a former live-in girl friend. Is that the kind of relationship you were thinking of?"

"No, not at all, Betty. I'm much more serious about us than that. I think we could have a very fine future together. But, we've only known each other a very short time, and, while I like you very much, that's not the same as living with each other. We're neither of us kids any more, and we're used to living our own lives, not sharing the same house."

Then, seeing something in Betty's expression, he continued, "If that old girl friend is bothering you, we called it quits some time ago. It was mutual. She lives in California now. So far I've done about all the talking."

"Yes, and that's the first time I've heard more than four or five words out of you at one time. Keep going. If things work out between us two, what do you conceive of as our relationship then? Other than weekend sailing?"

"Damn it, Betty, I thought I covered that pretty well, as far as I can, now. Let's hear what you think we can work out for ourselves."

"I think my feelings for you are more than just 'like'. I'm afraid I'm in love with you. I guess I was feeling a need for closure, and you're not ready for that. Let me make a suggestion. How would you feel if I moved in here for a very specific period, like two weeks? That might give us a fair idea of how we could get along together."

"That would be fantastic, if you'd do that, Betty! I think that might help us both to get our thoughts straight. When would you want to move in?"

"That possibility occurred to me before I left home, so I packed a few suitcases and left them. Whenever you're free from your job for a couple of hours, you could drive me to Boston and pick them up and bring them down here. How does that strike you?"

"Betty, I think you're wonderful! I can probably take tomorrow off. We'll drive up then. And I know a great restaurant in the North End. We can have lunch there. This is going to be great!"

CHAPTER XXVII

Three days later Dennis was sitting in his office going over a series of police reports when Sergeant Snow burst in. "Chief, you were right! Frank Barnes just told me he's ready to talk to you. Do you want me to bring him in?"

"No, take him in to the interviewing room. I'll meet you there in five minutes."

"Right, Chief."

Five minutes later Barnes was seated in a chair at the small table in the tiny interviewing room. Both Dennis and Snow were standing, looking down at him. Dennis began the questioning. "Okay, Frank, let's have it. You said you were ready to talk. So talk."

"Chief, are you sure you'll go to bat for me? I want your promise on that."

"All I can promise you is that I'll put in a good word for you with the DA's office. After that you'll have to work things out with them yourself."

"Well, I guess I can trust you."

"Get on with it, Frank, or I'll send you back to your cell."

"Okay, Chief. It all started about two or three days before the Blessing of the Fleet. This guy, Bill Phillips or something, he corners Joe Stabile and I on Commercial Street and tells us he might have a job for us. Well, you know the two of us are always in the market for honest work, so we says sure."

"Just skip the hearts and flowers, Frank; stick to the story."

"This guy, he tells us he wants us to take a boat out into the outer harbor, late at night the night of the Blessing, and pick up a package from another boat that'll meet us out there. We ain't supposed to talk to anybody, just pick up the package and row back to Saylor's and give Bill the package."

"And that was all?"

"Yeah, but when we get out in the harbor, one guy on the other boat says, 'Where's the envelope you're supposed to give me?' I tell him Bill never said nuthin' about no envelope. So he says, 'Hurry up and row back to shore and tell Bill we want that envelope, and we want him to bring it out. Understand?'

"So, Joe and me, we row back to Saylor's and tell Bill. So he gets in the boat with us; incidentally, that scow of Al Saylor's was damn heavy to row. And then we row back out to that other boat and Bill climbs on board that one and goes below.

"Right away we hear lots of loud talkin' and arguin', just like a married couple. Then it gets real quiet, and Joe and me, we're sitting there, wondering what's happening. Then two guys come out on deck, carrying something heavy. They dump it into our boat and their boat takes off like a big bird, out of the harbor."

"What did they dump into the boat? The package?"

"Yeah, but they also dumped Bill. And he looked like he was dead. And a bloody knife in a sheath."

"So then what happened?"

"Joe and me, we rowed back to the boat yard, ran into Al Saylor's office. He was there and we told him what happened. He told us to bring in the package. So I went out to the dory and picked up the package and left the body in the boat, and went back in to the office and gave the package to Al."

"Did you guys ever check to see if Phillips was really dead? Maybe he was still alive and you helped finish him off, so you could have what was in the package?"

"Aw, Chief! This is strictly straight stuff. I swear he was dead when they dropped him in our dory."

"All right, go on."

"Al takes the package and goes into his inside office. He's in there for about ten minutes and comes out without the package.

He tells me and Joe he has a job for us. He wants us to go out in his runabout with him, take the dory under tow, and when we get around into the bay, to let the dory go. He says the tide is running north, and the dory should go out into Massachusetts Bay and sink when the waves hit it.

" So we do that, go back to Al's dock and go back in the office. Al goes into his inner office and comes out with ten twenties and gives five to each one of us. He tells us to forget everything we seen tonight. Then, when we're ready to leave, he looks us over and tells us to go home and change our clothes, get rid of the old ones, and show our faces around town.

"So we did, and that's all, so help me God."

"Well, now. That's quite an interesting story. Sounds to me, though, like it needs some careful editing. Just as an example: what kind of boat did the package come from? What name and/or serial numbers did it have? Describe the men who were aboard her. Are you sure you left the package with Al Saylor? I think we'll let you sit in your cell and think about some answers for me."

Dennis walked to the door and handed Frank over to the patrolman who was standing outside it. "Make sure this guy and Joe Stabile don't get near each other."

Dennis walked slowly back to his office and picked up the phone. He asked Dot to put through a call to Sergeant Wallham. When he was connected he gave the sergeant a thumbnail sketch of Barnes's story, then said, "I guess the next step is to get Joe Stabile to give us his version. I think it would be very important for you to participate in that and be very involved with these two dainty birds."

The two set a date for the next morning to resume the questioning, this time with Joe Stabile as the honored guest, or rather, star performer.

CHAPTER XXVIII

The next day, Dennis, Sergeant Wallham and Sergeant Snow were seated on one side of the interview room. Dennis looked over to Sergeant Wallham. "I think it might be in order for you to do the questioning, at least to start with. You've read the transcript of Barnes's statement, so you're as up to date as I am, and this is really your case."

"Good enough. If you think I'm missing something as we go along, feel free to jump in."

The three were quiet until Joe Stabile was brought in and seated in the solitary chair on the opposite side of the table. "I'm Sergeant Wallham, of the State Police Detective Division. I believe you know these other two officers."

Joe nodded, and Wallham began. "We have a statement from your partner Frank Barnes that indicates that you both are closely involved in the murder of Bill Phillips and also in the delivery of a large amount of cocaine on the night of the Blessing of the Fleet.

"At this point, we'd like to hear your version of what happened that night. Believe me, things will go a lot easier for you if you cooperate with us. You've been read your rights the other day. Do you have any questions before we start?"

"First, tell me what Frank told you. Then I'll tell you my side."

"You're not in any position to lay down any conditions. We'll tell you how it's gonna go. Why don't you start at the beginning?"

"Okay, anybody got a cigarette?" Sergeant Snow looked questioningly at Wallham, who nodded. Snow then reached inside her uniform shirt pocket and drew out a pack of Marlboros and shook out one and handed it to Joe. Snow lit a match and helped Joe light his cigarette.

"This guy, the dead guy Bill, hired Frank and me to row a boat out to the outer harbor and pick up this package from a boat that would be out there."

"That was the night of the fleet blessing?"

"Yeah, he didn't want anybody to notice, and said nobody would, that night. Everybody would be busy partying, or just getting drunk."

"When did Phillips hire you to pick up the package?"

"A couple of weeks before." Joe looked around at the people sitting across the table from him. Seeing that none of them was going to say anything, he continued. "That night we went to Saylor's Boat Yard and tried to rent a skiff from him, but he wanted a lot of dough for anything decent, so we ended up taking out this old wooden dory that looked like it would crumble and sink any minute.

"Anyways, we rowed out and couldn't find any boat. So we waited around for a while. When the boat didn't show, we rowed back to Saylor's and met Bill and told him about the other boat not showin' up. Then Bill, he says to row him back out and he'll find that other boat, we must'a been waitin' in the wrong spot.

"So, out we goes again, this time with Bill. And we finally find the boat, way out, pick up the package, after Bill talks to the guys on the other boat, and row back to shore."

"And Bill was still alive when you rowed back to shore?"

Frank nodded and Wallham told him to answer out loud, the tape recorder won't hear him nod.

"Yep, he was still OK."

"Go on."

"We go into the yard office after we dock and tie up the boat. Al is there and him and Bill go into Al's inner office and come out a few minutes later without the package."

"Did you notice anything lying in the bottom of the dory?"

"Yeah, there was a box of rubbers, a pair of rubber gloves...."

"By rubbers, do you mean condoms?"

"No, like you use on lobster claws."

"Okay, go on."

"That's it."

"What happened after Bill and Al came out of the office?"

"We went down town and horsed around for a while and went home."

"That's a very interesting story, but it doesn't fit in with the facts we have."

"What do you mean?"

"Well, you and Frank were seen leaving Al's in Jack Brewer's taxi, wearing clothes that had blood on them. Then you came back a short while later and you had clean clothes on."

Silence, for several minutes, then Joe spoke up in a whiny voice, "You just gotta believe me, Frank and me, we didn't do no murder."

"So what did you do to get blood on your clothes?"

"A few minutes after we got back from meeting that boat, some guy comes in and joins Al and Bill in the inner office. Then, all hell breaks loose. We hear some furniture turn over, then a couple of seconds later it gets quiet in there. Then Al and this guy tell us there's been an accident, and that Bill has been stabbed by accident. Al wants us to take Bill's body out to the dory, also this knife and sheath. Says to row it out into the bay and he'll pick us up in his outboard and let the dory drift out into Mass. Bay. It's bound to sink in a couple of hours.

"So we done that, we come back here and Al gives us some money and tells us to get home, change our clothes and come back. He calls Jack Brewer and Jack comes over and takes us to my house. We change and Jack takes us back to Al's. Al tells us to go downtown and make like nothin' happened, maybe slash a tire to keep the cops busy. We take the package out and give it to Jack, and he drops us off in front of Town Hall."

"How much did Al give each of you?"

"A hundred and fifty."

"Who was the 'guy' who came in before Phillips got stabbed?"

"I dunno. I never seen him before."

"What did he look like?"

"I never noticed. It was dark in there and he just came and went fast and didn't say nuthin'."

"We'll get some mug shots for you to look over. We'll get the transcript typed up so you can sign it."

Joe was taken out and back to his cell. Wallham looked over at Dennis. "What do you think?"

"Interesting, the professor never mentioned another man going into Saylor's place. I think we might want to call him back in. We also better get Al Saylor and give him a thorough going over. Meet back here at two this afternoon?"

"Can I buy you guys lunch? On the state?"

"Thanks, but I think lunch is waiting for me at home." Sergeant Wallham looked questioningly at Sergeant Snow, who shrugged as if to say, 'Don't expect me to explain for him,' and the two of them walked out of the police station together.

Left alone, Dennis sighed, walked out and drove to his house.

As he drove along, Dennis's mind was a jumble of thoughts and feelings. *Damn, what have I got myself into? I used to be able to decide what I want to do on a moment's notice, or less. Now, if I want to go out for lunch with a couple of the guys, I either have to say no, or call Betty to tell her I won't be home for lunch, and then feel guilty about it.*

I'm not sure that the relationship, whatever it is, is worth giving up my freedom for. But I do love Betty and having her around is really nice. And we do have some great sex. I wish I could share my feelings with her, but I'm sure she'll only get upset, we'll end up having a fight, and then she'll either sulk, get real mad or even, maybe, walk out altogether.

I also wonder how Betty feels about all this. After all, she did leave her home, her friends to come down here. What does she do to occupy herself all day long while I'm at work, and part of lots of nights, too? Wish I knew a good shrink. But I know those guys; he'd just say, "Well, what do you think?"

And, at this point I'm doing a lousy job, especially with this Phillips murder. Seems like I can't concentrate on anything specific these days. I know what would help: take a couple of days off and get out on my boat. Think things through, not have to relate to anyone else. Try to come up with some direction for myself. Sigh. But that's impossible, what with everything that's going on. And I thought teaching in Roxbury was tough!

Dennis arrived at his house to find Betty packing.

"What's going on? Why are you packing?"

"I've decided this isn't working, so I'll be moving back to my room at the B&B. I think we both need a little breathing room, especially you. And if we continue this way, we'll never last. I can sense how hemmed in you are feeling, and I don't want to be a jailer."

"I'm sorry, Betty, I didn't think it showed. But you're right, we have to sort things out between us before we set ourselves up for a more intense relationship."

"I've thought this over and over. I even called my old therapist in Boston, and she agreed that we should cool it for a while. In the meantime, I've arranged to work as a volunteer at the Provincetown Museum, so that will keep me busy and out of mischief."

Dennis's expression brightened, "I guess I should have spoken up; we could have resolved this earlier. Are you sure that's what you want to do?"

"Yes, my mind's made up. We can still see each other as often as we both want, and there'll be less pressure on both of us."

They both grasped each other in a tight hug, then Betty said, "So, when are you going to invite me to go sailing?" She picked up her suitcases, asked, "Would you mind driving me?" and started out the door.

CHAPTER XXIX

That afternoon, back in Dennis's office, Sergeants Wallham and Snow were sitting discussing the Red Sox when Dennis walked in. He sat down behind his desk and looked over at the two sergeants, but particularly at Sergeant Wallham. "It seems to me we've been dragging our tails over this case for some time. Do you want to keep working together, or do you think you might manage more effectively on your own?"

"I've been wondering the same thing, and I think we've been working together fine. The thing is, we haven't been putting in all the time we should have with all these witnesses. I suggest we get them in, one at a time, until we come up with a whole story about exactly what happened that night, where when and how. And who was there and did what."

Dennis began rubbing his moustache, then searched around his desk until he found his supply of bubble gum. He offered some to the other two, who refused, not very gracefully, and then, after shoving a wad in his mouth, responded. "I realize I've been some lax about this case, but I think now we'd really better buckle down and show some results. I've got the Board of Selectmen on my back, and I'm sure you've been getting pressure from your higher-ups too."

Sergeant Wallham sighed and said, "You're right. I am really hearing from my captain about when we are going to resolve this whole case. So, if it's okay with you, why don't we get started?"

Dennis nodded. "I've told my men to get Al Saylor in the interview room, so I guess we can start with him. I guess you'll want to continue doing the questioning."

"Sure, but if either of you wants to jump in just go ahead." The three left the office and, just a couple of minutes later, entered the interview room where Al Saylor sat nervously puffing on a cigarette.

Dennis began, "Al, you know who Sergeant Snow and I are. This is Sergeant Wallham of the state police. He is in charge of this investigation of the murder of William Phillips. So far we haven't charged anyone with the crime, and we've brought you in to answer some questions. Sergeant Wallham will begin to do the questioning."

Wallham sat down across the table from Saylor and stared at him for a long minute, during which time Saylor began to squirm in his seat and lower his glance down toward the table. Wallham pushed an ashtray across the table to Saylor and said, "I want you to put out your cigarette."

Al did so with a shaking hand and seemed to shrink in his chair.

"A lot went on at your place the night of the fleet blessing. You start telling us exactly what happened, and we'll ask questions when we need to. Okay. Go ahead."

Al began to talk, in a very weak voice, and was quickly interrupted by Sergeant Wallham. "We're taping this and you're not talking loud enough, so start over and louder this time."

"The night of the Blessing of the Fleet, these two guys, Joe and Frank...."

"Joe who and Frank who?"

"Joe Stabile and Frank Barnes. They came by my yard and wanted to rent a dinghy, but they didn't want to pay what any of my dinghies cost to rent. So I told them they could have that old wooden dory for what they wanted to pay. We went out to the dock and...."

"What time was that?"

"About nine-thirty or so. We went out to the dock and I helped them get the dory set and gave them a push away from the dock. Of course, after I collected for the dory rental."

He looked questioningly at Wallham, who nodded, then Al began again.

"Shortly after that this guy Bill Phillips comes in and asks me, 'Did those two jokers show up and rent one of your dinghies?' So I tell him, yes and he sits down and we chat for a while and then the jokers show up and tell Bill they been out in the harbor and there ain't no other boat they could find out there and what are they supposed to do?

"Then Bill tells them to row him out in the dory, he'll find the damned boat. So out they go, looking for that boat, whatever it is, and I went back in my office to work on some bills."

"Do you have any idea what they wanted with that boat?"

"It was just Bill Phillips wanted to meet with that other boat. Turned out later that they collected a package from the boat, all wrapped up in waterproof wrapping paper. Heavy, too."

"What was in the package?"

"Damned if I know, Sergeant."

"You expect us to believe that? Where is the package now? We were led to believe you have the package, or at least it was left with you that night."

"No, those other guys took it with them."

"Which other guys?"

"Bill and Joe and Frank, those guys."

At this time, Sergeant Wallham caught Dennis's eye and pointed to the door. Leaving Saylor in the company of Sergeant Snow, they marched out of the room and gathered down the hallway. "He's lying in his teeth," said Wallham. "I think we're going to charge him and hold him, at least on a charge of possession and work him over on a suspicion of murder."

"I agree completely," said Dennis. "Will you be transferring him to your jail?

"No, not until we get the proper arrest warrants. In the meantime I'd like to get some DNA samples—without a court order, if you know what I mean—and get them off to the lab for matching. Also, anything you may have on those other two. Okay?"

"Sure. I'll get to work on it right away."

They trooped back into the room, where Al Saylor was looking even more anxious than before, if that were possible.

"Al, we're going to book you on possession of dangerous drugs and suspicion of homicide." Wallham then read Saylor his rights and then asked him, "Do you have any questions?"

"I want to see a lawyer."

"Do you have one?"

"Yeah, my wife's uncle Arthur."

"Okay we'll let you call him. For now we don't have any more to talk about until you see your lawyer."

Dennis opened the door, looked back at Snow and, pointing a finger at Al, said, "Book him."

CHAPTER XXX

Professor Toro, this is Sergeant Wallham, of the State Police Homicide Section; this is Sergeant Snow, of the Provincetown Police Homicide Section, and the rest are officers of both departments. We have your testimony that you were parked outside Saylor's Boat Yard on the night of the Blessing of the Fleet, and that you reported seeing several people move in and out of that office there. Sergeant Wallham has some questions about what you saw."

The group was seated in the former viewing room of the former funeral home that served a multitude of functions in what was now Provincetown Police Headquarters. All seven men, as well as Sergeant Snow, were seated around a large conference table, which nearly filled the room. A tape recorder sat noticeably out on the table recording the proceedings.

"Professor, I know you gave Chief Dawes a report of what you were able to remember of what you saw that night, but I'd like for you to tell it to us again, and try hard to remember everything you saw as you sat there in your Jeep that night."

"Well, I'm not happy about all these questions. But that night I came into town to buy some cigarettes and to meet with a former student of mine, with whom I had an appointment to meet at Saylor's Boat Yard at ten o'clock."

"Did you meet with him?"

"No, he never showed up."

"You told Chief Dawes that you saw two men carry a package that appeared to be heavy into the yard office. You then heard talking from the office, then the two men you had seen bringing in the package leaving in a taxi. And that you left right after that. Is that right?"

"What do you mean, is that right? I told the chief the truth."

"And you drove right home?'

"Yes."

"Anybody see you after that, that night?"

"No, there was no one at my home when I got there, and I went right to bed."

"Professor, do you have any idea why William Phillips's fingerprints are on the passenger door handle and the dashboard of your car?"

"I don't think I'll answer any more questions. I want to call my lawyer."

"No need, you're free to go. But don't leave this area without checking with the chief, here." And they all got up and left.

CHAPTER XXXI

Once again the police group was assembled in the meeting room. Dennis turned to Sergeant Wallham. "Do you want to begin, then the rest of us can chime in when it's appropriate?"

"Sure thing. We seem to have a lot to catch up on, so why don't we start with all that? It appears to me that we have at least four likely candidates for the honor of being our most probable suspect. Those two favorite characters of yours, Dennis, Stabile and Barnes. Failing them, we've got Al Saylor. That reminds me, Dennis, have you alerted the ATF people yet?"

"Yeah, I've been in touch with the Boston office, and they're sending a squad down here, but they couldn't be sure when that would happen. We'll probably find out when they get here."

"I'm sure they're working on it now, even though they're not here. Well, to continue, finally we have the professor. He's not a sweet-smelling character, but, aside from those fingerprints on his Jeep and the Phillips' DNA in a couple of places, there isn't much evidence linking him directly with the murder. If this was an Agatha Christie novel, we'd be getting them all together in a mansion living room on a stormy night and forcing the murderer to confess. Any baronial mansions around here, Sergeant Snow?"

"Are you sure you're not leaving out Jim Easton and Jack Brewer, *Sergeant* Wallham?" was Snow's response, as she uncrossed her legs and leaned further back in her chair. "We can probably trot out a few more suspects for your grand inquisitorial session. I think we can find the mansion for you also."

Sergeant Wallham gave her an exaggerated frown and continued. "I think it's time to get the professor in here, with his lawyer, and either confirm or dismiss him as our chief suspect. I also think this group is a bit too big to continue right now, so I'd like to suggest that we limit our side to you, Dennis, Sergeant Snow and myself. Okay?"

Dennis turned to Snow. "What do you think, Janet?"

"I agree. I'd also like to be the first to question him. I have the feeling that he considers himself quite a man for the ladies. We might get along a little faster with him that way."

A big smile lit up Sergeant Wallham's entire face as she was saying this. "That's great, although if I was the one to suggest that, you'd have me up on charges of sexual harassment within five minutes."

Her response didn't take five minutes. "Just be careful. I think I saw you thinking about asking me to get coffee for the three of us a while ago. But, let's get him in. I saw his lawyer in the office a few minutes before we started."

The other four officers rose at a nod from Wallham and walked out of the room. A few minutes later, Professor Toro and his attorney entered the room and Dennis ushered them to seats across the large table from the policemen. The chief then introduced the two sergeants and himself to the lawyer, who identified himself as William Swiss, Esquire.

They all sat down and Sergeant Snow, to the obvious surprise of both the professor and his lawyer, said, "I have a few questions for you, professor." As she said this, she smiled warmly at both of them and began.

"Professor Toro, would you tell us what your relationship was with Mr. Phillips?"

Toro glanced over at the lawyer, who nodded. Then Toro began, "He was a student in one of my classes a couple of years ago, then he dropped out of school. But before he left, he got involved with a girl who accused him of date rape. He asked me to talk to the young lady and try to convince her not to press charges."

"And did you?"

"I did. At first she was quite negative about the whole business, but after I told her that if she did press charges she would find the campus a rather hostile environment, she agreed not to pursue it. Young people don't generally approve of girls making accusations like that. So, finally, she saw that I was entirely right and agreed not to proceed with the charges."

"And was that the end of it?"

"Yes, for the time. Phillips was very grateful and assured me that if I should ever need help of any kind, he would be happy to be of service."

"Did he specify what kind of service he was prepared to offer?"

At that point Toro looked questioningly at his lawyer, who said to Wallham, "I want to consult privately with my client before we continue."

Wallham gave him a quick, "Okay, let us know when you're finished." The three officers rose and left the room.

While they were waiting, Dennis and the two sergeants filled cups with coffee and sipped slowly.

"You're doing fine so far. I think you have him worried a bit. Wonder why he wanted to talk to the lawyer." This from Wallham.

Before Janet Snow could answer, the door to the room opened and the attorney poked his head out and told the police that his client was ready to continue.

They filed back into the interview room and seated themselves. "Before we were interrupted, I asked you what kind of service Bill Phillips was prepared to offer you. Have you decided to answer my question?"

"Yes, Sergeant, er, Snow is it? Phillips was an enterprising young man, although not always in the right direction, if you get my drift."

"I'm not sure I get your drift. Would you please be more specific?"

"Well, the word on campus was that he was involved in drugs. He was said to be peddling pot and things like that. Of course I was never interested in using any of that stuff."

"Then did you have any other need for help that Bill Phillips was able to provide?"

"Yes, a current graduate student of mine, Robert Benson, was becoming difficult to advise, so I thought that Bill Phillips, who was a cousin of Benson's, could help convince him, Benson, that I was looking out primarily for his interests. So, when Benson came out to Cape Cod to follow me, I asked Phillips to intervene."

"But, Professor, when we interviewed Robert Benson and Diana Wellman, they both insisted that Robert came to the Cape to find Diana and get her away from you. Okay, let's move on. The night of the Blessing, you told Chief Dawes you drove into town to buy cigarettes. You aren't a smoker, are you?"

"No, but I was very upset over the fracas that Benson caused at my house that afternoon, and I thought a smoke might calm my nerves."

"You didn't buy any cigarettes, did you?"

"No, I couldn't find any stores open."

"Professor, on the night of the Blessing of the Fleet, in Provincetown, Massachusetts, you couldn't find a place to sell you a pack of cigarettes? You later told Chief Dawes that you had an appointment to meet Bill Phillips, but that he didn't show up. Do you have a Professor Toro alumni club here on Cape Cod?"

"Well, I do have many former students who think I was one of the best professors they had at Brookline University."

"Let's get back to reality. You have said that you sat in your Jeep outside Saylor's Boat Yard for quite some time after Easton failed to show up. At what time did Bill Phillips appear?"

"I never said he appeared."

"Are you saying it now, that he never appeared and sat in the front passenger seat of your vehicle on the night of Sunday, June 28th? And that you and he didn't hold a conversation there in said vehicle, and further that you and he didn't have some quarrel, and that you didn't struggle and that you didn't kill him?"

"There was a lot going on in my life at that time, and I was confused when the Chief, here, was questioning me. Actually he did show up and we sat in my car and talked for a while."

"Go on."

"I wanted his help in convincing his cousin Robert Benson that Robert should cooperate with me on his thesis."

"And what did Phillips say?"

"He said that he and Robert were not on friendly terms, and that he had a lot of other things going on in his own life right then, and he couldn't spare the time. I reminded him of his commitment to me, but he said it would have to be on hold for a while."

"What happened then?"

"I was about to get nasty with him, when suddenly the door to the boat yard office opened, two men came out and got into a taxi that was waiting a short way down the street. Bill jumped out of my Jeep and ran into the office. I waited a while and then I left and went back to my cottage."

At this point Sergeant Snow glanced at Sergeant Wallham, who nodded briefly, and the three officers rose and walked out the door. Wallham paused briefly at the door and said to Mr. Swiss, "We'll be back in a few minutes. Don't go away."

About five minutes later, Sergeant Wallham, Dennis and Sergeant Snow entered the room. This time Sergeant Wallham acted as spokesperson for the group. "Mr. Swiss, we're going to hold your client as a material witness. We'll have him moved to a state facility and notify you of his whereabouts so that you can visit him when you wish. You may have a few minutes to talk now."

The three left the room and met in Dennis's office.

CHAPTER XXXII

Well, what do you think?" This was directed at Janet Snow and Dennis, but primarily aimed at Snow.

"I think he's our guy. I'm willing to bet he didn't leave after Phillips went inside Saylor's office. I'd bet he followed Phillips right into the office and was the guy that Barnes and Stabile talked about. I also think he is involved in the drug situation and may still be calling the shots on that side."

"I tend to agree with Janet," Dennis said, "I think it would be a good idea to have Stabile and Barnes get a look at Toro, individually, of course, and see what they have to say. What do you think, Sergeant?"

"I think, first, that I'd like you to call me Tom. Then, I agree with both of you that he's our prime suspect. The question in my mind is, are we ready to bring the DA's office into this now? Do we feel that we have the prospects of a solid case for him? What evidence should we be looking for to build up our case? Sorry, I guess that's more than one question."

There occurred a period of silence that lasted several minutes. None of the three appeared to want to answer those questions. Finally, Dennis spoke up. "How would you feel about sounding the DA out about his opinion? It seems to me that we have a lot of evidence piled up here, and he ought to have some say about what direction we take now."

Deep sigh. "You're right, he's the man...excuse me, Janet, the person to talk to now. I'll get back to you soon." And out he went, along with his crew.

Dennis looked over inquiringly at Janet Snow.

She shook her head and said, "I don't want to talk about it now. I need to try to straighten things out in my mind."

"Okay, it's time to quit for the day. See you Monday morning. Tomorrow's Sunday and I'm taking the day off to take Betty sailing." They walked out together.

CHAPTER XXXIII

I f you want me to help in any way, you'd better tell me just what you want me to do. This is my first time on a sailboat." Betty, happy, yet simultaneously a bit anxious, was seated in the cockpit of Dennis's boat *Khamsin* while the boat was at a mooring in Provincetown Harbor.

At the same time, Dennis was busy going through all the routines of getting the boat ready for a day's sailing. He untied the piece of line laced around the furled-up genoa sail, untied the ties that held the mainsail close against the main boom, all except one. Then he hanked the main halyard to the head of the mainsail. While he was accomplishing these chores, he kept up a steady commentary aimed at making Betty an instant sailor.

Finally deciding that he was ready to leave the mooring, Dennis flicked on a switch that operated a blower in the bilge to exhaust any fuel fumes that might be there. Then when he decided there were no longer any fumes, Dennis shut off the blower and turned the key in the switch, starting the small engine which served as auxiliary power for the twenty-eight foot sloop.

When he was satisfied that the engine was running smoothly, Dennis said to Betty, "Here, this stick I'm going to have you hold is called a tiller. Just hold it steady until I get back here to the cockpit and I'll tell you what to do next." He then moved forward to the bow, reached down and grasped a line with a buoy attached to it, released it from the cleat holding it to the deck, and dropped both line and buoy into the water. He then walked as quickly as he could back to the cockpit, shifted the engine into gear and put his hands over Betty's on the tiller and gently moved it to where he wanted it.

As soon as the boat cleared the harbor, Dennis said to Betty, "Can you feel where the wind is coming from?"

"Yes." Betty pointed in the direction where she thought it was coming from.

"That's right. Now, keep the boat pointing right into the wind while I hoist the sails."

Betty complied and Dennis released the last tie on the mainsail and wound two turns of the main halyard around a winch near the base of the mainmast. He inserted a winch handle into a slot on the winch and began turning the handle rapidly, which caused the mainsail to slide upward through a slot in the mast until the sail was completely open. Dennis then tied the halyard around a cleat on the mast, removed the handle from the winch and inserted it into a plastic pocket on the side of the cockpit.

He looked over at Betty to see how she was doing at the tiller, and everything seemed to be under control, so Dennis began pulling on a line he called a jib sheet, after first untying the furling line which had kept the jib furled. As soon as the jib was completely unfurled and was caught by the wind, Dennis moved over and took the tiller from Betty.

He turned the boat slightly away off the wind and tightened another sheet, which pulled the boom and the base of the sail closer to the center of the boat. Almost instantly the boat began to lean away from the wind and pick up speed. Dennis reached down and shifted the engine into neutral gear and then shut it off.

As *Khamsin* began to heel over more, Betty began to feel somewhat anxious. Dennis, seeing this and recognizing a need on her part for some reassurance, sat down next to her and had her hold the tiller with him. He began explaining why sailboats heel on some points of sail, and tried to convince her that there was absolutely no danger when that happened.

After a while Betty began to feel more comfortable with the boat's heeling and more confident in her ability not to make it capsize. "Let me see if I can sail it by myself. How do I steer it?"

"With the tiller. If you want to turn to the right, called

starboard on a boat, you pull the tiller toward you, since you're sitting on the left side now. That's called the port side. If you want to turn to port, push the tiller away from you. Only do it a little bit at a time."

Betty tried to follow Dennis's directions, obviously concentrating very hard, but making the sailboat follow a zigzag pattern of wake behind it as she alternately pushed and pulled at the tiller. Finally she visibly made a decision. "Dennis, it's time for you to take over."

With that she let go of the tiller, and, fortunately, Dennis was able to grab it and return it to its proper direction before anything untoward occurred.

Betty asked Dennis whether she could go up to the foredeck, and he said "Sure, but take a floatation cushion with you and hold onto it while you're up there."

Very carefully, she made her way to the foredeck, which she had referred to as "up front" and sat down resting her back against the main mast. At first, the jib sheet resting against the mast began to flutter, so Betty moved it up and over her head and let it lie across her lap. She found it difficult to focus on any particular sight for long; there were so many beautiful sights to see. To her left were the highlands of Truro, and, in the distance, of Wellfleet. To her right, *That's starboard,* Betty thought, was a huge expanse of aquamarine tinted water with reflections of the sunlight off the crests of the small waves into which *Khamsin* was heading.

The gentle up-and-down motion of the boat finally had its effect on Betty, and she became quite drowsy. Seeing this Dennis called out, "Honey, you'd better come back here if you're going to take a nap. We don't want to have to hold a man overboard drill out here. Besides, you're no man!"

Betty quickly made her way back to the cockpit and sat next to Dennis, leaning slightly against him as he steered the boat. Just then his cell phone rang and he answered, "Yeah, we're out on my boat." He listened intently for a moment. "I guess we could be back in by around three." Another pause. "Oh I wouldn't want to miss that! Just stick him in an empty office 'til we get back in. And don't let anybody talk to him."

He switched off his phone, turned *Khamsin* around and headed back to Provincetown harbor.

CHAPTER XXXIV

After they had returned *Khamsin* to her mooring, snugged her down and dinghied to the dock, Betty and Dennis stood momentarily on the dock. "Can I drop you off someplace, Betty? I have to get back to my office very soon, but I can still drop you at your B&B."

"No, thanks, but it's still a beautiful day, and I'd love to just walk around for a while. This is such a fascinating place."

"Great idea! Dinner tonight? There are still a few places we haven't tried together."

"Okay, would you pick me up at about seven-thirty?"

"It's a date."

A few minutes later Dennis entered his office. He got Dot on the intercom. "Is Janet around anywhere? I want to speak with her before I talk to our young friend."

"She's in the building, Chief. I'll get her for you."

"Thanks, Dot."

A few minutes later Janet entered Dennis's office. "You wanted to see me, Dennis?"

"Yeah, sit down for a minute. I'd like to sound you out on your feelings about Robert Benson before we interview him. It drives me wild to hear his mother call him Bobby. It sounds as if she's trying to keep him a baby."

"Well, from the few minutes I spent with him, and getting a look at his girlfriend, I'd say he's no baby."

"We have no accounting from him as to his activities after he dropped Ms. Wellman off at her motel. What approach do you think we should take with him?"

"Dennis, is that your subtle way of asking me to do the

questioning? I'm well aware of your relationship with his mother, and it won't get you any brownie points if you give her son the third degree."

"Gee, Janet, thanks for offering. I knew I could count on you." Dennis stepped out and asked one of the officers to bring Robert Benson to the meeting/interview/conference/ room, which had been the viewing room/funeral room when the building had been occupied by a funeral home.

CHAPTER XXXV

A few minutes later, Robert was ushered in unceremoniously by the officer.

Right away, in spite of his commitment to Janet, Dennis spoke up, "Nice of you to come down and see us. We hope we haven't interfered with your research too much."

Janet Snow gave Dennis a cautionary look that said, "Go easy, Dennis, we want this young man to be cooperative."

"I'm sorry, I thought I had your permission to stay at the dig until it was shut down. I came here as soon as it was."

Janet jumped in with "Okay, Robert. Now that you're here there are quite a few questions we have that you might be able to answer." Robert nodded. "We're going to tape record this interview. If you want a lawyer present, say so now."

"No. I have nothing to hide from you."

"Robert, please tell us what you did on the night of the Blessing of the Fleet, from the time you dropped Ms. Wellman at her motel."

"As you probably know, Diana and I had just had a very big blowup at Toro's dune shack, and I was still burning, at her and at Toro. So I drove down and parked along Bradford Street. I knew Bill Phillips, my cousin, would be at John's Cafe, and when I was real mad at Diana, I had given her engagement ring to Bill to try to sell for me. Even though I was still mad, I thought the two of us would probably get back together and I was hoping to give the ring back to her.

"When I got there they told me that Bill had just left, and that they had seen him wearing a diamond ring on a strip of rawhide around his neck. Nobody there seemed to know where he had been heading, except that someone recalled his making a date to meet Jack Brewer at Saylor's Boat Yard at ten or ten-thirty that night. Then I went to my mom's hotel to find out what was going on with her, but she had gone out to dinner with the chief, here."

"Tell us about later that night. What were you doing after about nine o'clock?"

I had dinner at a small place up on Commercial Street, Bayshore or Bayside, I think it's called."

"Bayside Betsy, do you mean?"

"Yeah, I guess that's it."

"Then what?"

"I kinda hung around the bar, had a couple of drinks, then walked to Saylor's boat yard to meet Bill and get my ring back."

"Did you meet him?"

"When I got there, there was no one around. That was around nine-fifteen or so. Then I saw a Jeep park just a bit down the street, and the driver just sat there. Then I saw a couple of rough-looking guys go in to the yard office, then, a few minutes later, go out on the dock and row away, then, some time later, row back to the dock and go into the office again."

"How much later was it when they returned?"

"About half an hour. Then they went out again, this time it looked like Bill was with them. Then they came back about fifteen minutes later and went into the office again."

"When they came back and went into the office, were they carrying anything?"

"Yeah, one of them was carrying what looked like a heavy package."

"Did you try to talk to Bill at any time while this was going on?"

"No, it looked like he was plenty busy, and I didn't like the looks of those two other guys."

"So, then what happened?"

"Bill came out and got into the Jeep that was parked there. While he was in the Jeep, the two guys came out and got into a taxi that had come up, and they drove away. Then they came back a few minutes later, and went back in the yard office. Just then, Bill came busting out of the Jeep and ran into the office.

"As soon as he got inside, the driver of the Jeep got out of the car and also went in to the office. Was I surprised when it turned out to be Professor Toro! I hung around for a while, then went back to my room, thinking I didn't want to get mixed up in whatever was going on in there. It certainly didn't look kosher to me."

"What else?"

"The next morning I met Diana for breakfast, then I thought it would be a good idea to drive down to Eastham where the dig was, and see if I could be allowed to finish my research there. I spoke to the professor in charge there and he said I could, so I drove back here, picked up my things, and returned to Eastham. I didn't tell Diana. I thought she'd try to keep me here."

Dennis interrupted the dialogue. "Son, I wish you'd told us all this a lot sooner. You caused a lot of problems around here by disappearing like that." Dennis turned to the sergeant and said, "Do you have any more questions for this fugitive from justice?"

"No, Chief, but I think we'll want him to stay here in Provincetown. There's no need for him to go anywhere else for a while."

Benton got up and walked out. Dennis turned to Janet Snow and said, "We'd better get this information to Tom Wallham right away. You did a great job with Robert." They both walked out of the room.

CHAPTER XXXVI

Dennis picked up his phone after the second ring. "Yes, Dot, what is it?"

"It's Sergeant Wallham on line 1 for you."

"Thanks, Dot. Hi, Tom, this is Dennis."

"Dennis, I want to thank you for that fax with the interview of Robert Benton you just sent me. I think what young Benton told you goes along with the ID those two reprobates, Barnes and Stabile, confirmed when you showed them pictures of the professor. It's pretty definite, that wraps up the case we have against him, now. At least the DA thinks we'll get him on a Murder Two rap.

"That's great, Tom! Anything else new?"

"We also heard from the DEA. According to them, the professor was the head of a group of his former students, importing cocaine and other lovely stuff. Apparently he was blackmailing the former students to make them cooperate with him. But the joke was on all of them this time. After we got confessions from Brewer, Stabile and Barnes, it turned out the package the fight was about only contained a white powder we found out later was baking soda. Seems their source was out to shaft them after their last screw up."

"That's wonderful! I guess I'm off the case. All I have to do for the little bit of summer that's left is just run my department, and take care of the summer folks. I might even get in a few more days of sailing.

"Well, Tom, I think you've done an excellent job with this case. I hope it will earn you a boost in your standing with the state. And I've enjoyed working with you. And, I'm sure, so has Janet."

"Please say goodbye to her for me. I know I've enjoyed working with both of you. And, by the way, if things don't work out between you and the Benton woman and the sergeant's still around....

"I know exactly what you mean, but no way! I'm her supervisor, and it wouldn't be ethical *or* practical."

"Okay, have a good, uneventful summer."

"You too." And they both hung up.

CHAPTER XXXVII

Come on in, Dennis. Here, have a seat." This invitation was from Charlie Perry, principal of the elementary school in Provincetown.

Dennis sat obediently, looked at Perry questioningly, and remained silent.

"I wanted to let you know that the School Committee unanimously approved your appointment as a teacher in the Provincetown Elementary School, starting August 23." Perry then mentioned a figure that Dennis would receive as salary, considerably lower than that he had earned as police chief.

"Well, I guess I'll have to arrange to rob a bank occasionally to make up the difference," said Dennis.

"You probably know a few fellows who could give you lessons," rejoined Perry.

The two then spent some time discussing what the job would entail and arranged for Dennis to go through some of the procedures involved. "Dennis, I wish you luck, I'm sure you have the skill, and you're going to do an excellent job."

"Thanks, Charlie, I'll do my best."

"May I get personal for a minute, Dennis?"

"Sure, go ahead."

"Dennis, we can't have you chewing that rotten bubble gum when you're in the classroom! I'd recommend you give it up altogether."

"Wow, if I'd thought this job was going to entail a lot of sacrifices, I'd have reconsidered taking it in the first place. Well, anything for the kids. Wouldn't want any of them picking up that terrible habit."

Charlie Perry proceeded to give Dennis some further instructions and information about the job, and, soon after, they shook hands and Dennis left.

About a week later, Dennis and Betty were having dinner in The Front Room, a fine restaurant on Commercial Street. "So it looks like I'll be quitting my job as chief. I've made all the arrangements with the principal to begin teaching in the elementary school here in P'town. The kids here deserve me as much as the ones in Boston did, and I was never really happy in the job of Police Chief."

"I'm sorry you didn't discuss all that with me before you made all your arrangements. I've been finding living here to be almost suffocating. There's practically nothing here that interests me, except for a few galleries and museums, and I think I've worn out my welcome in those places. It would have been great if you had applied for a job in one of the better schools in Boston, or even a good private school. I'm sure they would have welcomed you warmly. I guess you know what this all means."

"I guess it means neither of us wants to live in the other one's back yard."

"Dennis, I'm sorry it seems to be over between us, but it's been good for me. I've been learning how to get along on my own much better, and you've been a help with that." As she said this, Dennis winced. "And now I'm ready to get on with my life in Brookline."

"I'm sure I'm going to be busy full-time with my work in school. It's been a long time since I taught a class, so I have a lot of catching up to do. I don't think I'll have a lot of time for a social life, at least for the first year. I'm sorry things didn't work out between us."

"Dennis, you know, I thought that if the two of us were to break up, I would be heartbroken, but, now that it's happening, I'm not really that much upset."

They finished their meal with very little further conversation. Dennis walked Betty to her B&B, kissed her on the cheek, hesitated a moment, then hugged her, and said "Good luck, Betty. If you ever need me, for anything, please get in touch." He turned and walked away without looking back.

A short while later, the phone rang at Dennis's home. "Hello?"

" Is that you, Dennis?"

"Yes, Janet, it's me."

"Why didn't you tell me you were resigning, and that you sent the chairman of the Board of Selectmen a letter recommending me for the chief's job six weeks ago?"

"Because, at that time I wasn't sure of where I was going. But it's all settled now. You're talking to Dennis Dawes the teacher. And I hope I'm talking to Chief Snow."

"Dennis, I sure hope you'll do as well in that job as you've done here in the PPD. And they have to interview about four candidates, but I've been assured that the whole board is rooting for me."

"Janet, there's a reason I'm quitting that job, in addition to all the ones you know of. It struck me that you and I could never have the kind of relationship I'd like us to have as long as I was your boss. Do you follow me? And would you be interested?"

"I don't know. I was thinking, if I get the chief job, I could hire you part time to supplement your teaching salary. But I wouldn't be able to, under the circumstances you're suggesting."

"In that case, forget what I suggested. I wouldn't want to pass up that part- time cop's job. I guess I'd better look elsewhere."

"Dennis Dawes, I'm coming over there right now. And don't forget, I carry a gun!"

AFTERWORD

Even a cursory examination of most bookstore shelves would indicate that there is no dearth of murder mysteries for even the most voracious addict. The most current trend among mystery writers seems to follow a formula: once having written a story featuring an appealing mystery solver, be that solver a real detective or a talented amateur whose day job is in another field, they continue to write stories using the same cast of characters, or, at least, the same main character. And, make no mistake, many of these series turn out to be very successful, financially if not in literary style.

So, to me, the challenge was not to produce another first in a series that would bring a modest success in the marketplace and an author's name that would be on the tongue tip of millions of mystery fans. I have no negative feelings toward money. My motivation was elsewhere. I suppose, to put it as clearly as I can, what I had in mind was the creation of a mystery story that is almost the direct opposite.

First of all, the main character of this book is not your typical hero. He is frequently indecisive, unassertive, sloppy in dress and action, and is generally less than totally successful in his crime-solving efforts. He goes from one abortive stab at a job as a teacher to another as a policeman, to another as chief of police, then back to teacher again. His relationships with women seem to be limited to employer-employee, or ones that don't seem to involve much commitment on his part. In fact, the only commitment he seems to be willing to make is to sailing, and note that he brags that his sailboat is rigged so that he can sail it single-handed.

Second, what is the locale for most of the book? Cape Cod

is like an arm stretching out into the Atlantic Ocean for seventy-five miles and ending in a hook that is the town of Provincetown, affectionately known throughout the area as P'town, either with or without the apostrophe. This community, formerly made up of Portuguese fishing families, but now a busy and thriving tourist center, alternately shrinks in the winter to a small number of residents. In the summer, it explodes with a mighty influx of tourists, vacationers, artists and art seekers, gay and lesbian couples and groups, and service people to take care of the rest of the arrivals. The last Sunday in June is celebrated as the day of the Blessing of the Fleet, which consists of the passing of the boats of the fishing fleet past the end of the wharf, to be blessed individually by the bishop, along with religious observance in church in the morning and picnics and liquid celebration on boats and beaches in the late afternoon.

What makes this holiday unique for Provincetown is that, as opposed to other occasions such as Memorial Day, July Fourth, and Labor Day, which draw large crowds of visitors, the Blessing of the Fleet is celebrated mostly by the year-round residents of the town. To have a murder committed on this holiday, a day usually devoted to joyous observance, is, in itself, ironic.

In their attempts to solve the crime, the police, including squads from the local, state and federal police, seem rather desultory, in no hurry to reach a solution, and more interested in the process than its results. The police chief seems more interested in his romance with a visitor to the Cape who is tangentially involved in the murder, than in solving it. As it turns out, he has to have the solution explained to him by a member of the state police, rather than being part of the solution.

Part of the action in the story takes place at Brookline University, a wholly fictional institution not that different in nature from many actual institutions of higher learning that are undergoing some of the throes of self-examination, self-upgrading and, occasionally, self-aggrandizement. The fact that this institution's self study is somehow related to a murder in a distant community is not different from many occurrences in real life.

None of the characters in the book is taken from real life, except for one who shall remain nameless, as protection from being associated with some of the other characters. It is possible that, unconsciously, some of them may resemble, perhaps even closely, some people I have encountered in my lifetime. If so, then the resemblance to any person, living or dead... and so on.

To sum up, what I had in mind in the writing of this book was to create an existential mystery, in which the protagonists—and the antagonists for that matter—are no more effective and successful, nor any more ineffectual or unsuccessful than most of us in real life. But mostly we manage to get by.